To dear Sue, Enjoy! ♡ Jane Williams Le Cerf x

About the Author

Jane Williams Le Cerf was born in 1969. She grew up in Reading and currently lives in Bedfordshire. Jane trained as a secretary and progressed to personal assistant work for CEOs including Arthur Andersen, The Royal Television Society and Nestlé Europe. During this time, Jane undertook five diplomas, including; Social Science, Psychology and Career Counselling. Jane became a lecturer at Hammersmith, Kensington & Chelsea Colleges and was responsible for writing and delivering their Student Induction Programme which is still in use today. At 28, Jane worked for a famous royal family. *Falling For Wonderlust* is based on that experience.

For

Sébastién.
Fleur, Théo, Félix.
Mum and Dad.

All my love, always.

Jane Williams Le Cerf

FALLING FOR WONDERLUST

AUSTIN MACAULEY
PUBLISHERS LTD.

A CIP catalogue record for this title is available from the British Library.

ISBN 9781785548437 (Paperback)
ISBN 9781785548444 (Hardback)
ISBN 9781785548451 (E-Book)

www.austinmacauley.com

First Published (2016)
Austin Macauley Publishers Ltd.
25 Canada Square
Canary Wharf
London
E14 5LQ

Acknowledgments

Thanks to:

Gary Eason, Sue Coy & Vicky Rees.

He who binds to himself a joy
Does the winged life destroy;
But he who kisses the joy as it flies
Lives in eternity's sunrise.

William Blake

Contents

Wonderlust….definition: A word to describe the stage in a relationship or phase of love when you are not sure if you are lusting after or actually in love with someone.

Chapter One

The Advert

Vivienne sat nursing her filter soya venti at Starbucks on Chiswick High Road. She had left her desk at the Barley Mow Centre unable to stop the tears that had overcome her. Everything was becoming too much. On her doormat that morning, she had received another letter from her solicitor informing her that her soon-to-be ex-husband Timothy had failed yet again to attend Court and was now facing a subpoena charge, with a potential short stay at Her Majesty's pleasure. The satisfaction of knowing he would suffer just a little was overshadowed by the bill staring at her for a further £5,000 for legal fees. The debt was now £16,000. Vivienne might win the legal battle suing Timothy on wife abuse charges, but it was proving a financial torture as well as an emotional one. On top of this, she had arrived at her office to find another letter of doom informing her of company liquidation and attached to it by way of a black plastic coated paperclip, her last pay cheque. Her boss had not even bothered to inform her that the company was in dire straits and that the bank no longer wanted to support their overdraft and, not wanting to face the music, had ran off to Barbados for a month in the sun.

Wiping the tears away, Vivienne leant over to the table opposite and retrieved a copy of the Times newspaper that had just been abandoned by another customer. She may as well start looking for another job. In the 'crème-de-la-crème' section, an advert screamed out at her.

Required

A degree educated, well presented Personal Assistant/companion required for the Chair of a large multi-national company based in London.

The ability to speak French and a willingness to travel at short notice is essential.

Must be single and without dependents. Maximum 30 years of age.

£+ High rate of pay.

Tel: 0207 000 1998

Tearing the advertisement out of the newspaper, Vivienne stuffed it into her briefcase and headed for her car.

*

Vivienne couldn't sleep that night and tossed and turned a thousand times. She knew she would not rest until she had applied for the job.

At nine o'clock on the dot the next morning, Vivienne hastily dialled the number written on the advertisement before she could change her mind. An indifferent sounding young woman answered the phone and rattled off the same information she must have given out a thousand times that week.

"Send in your CV, a covering letter outlining why you think you are suitable for the position and a recent passport photograph. The standard of applications are extremely high and we have already received in over seven hundred CVs, so if you are not successful, we will not get back to you. Sorry." She rang off in the most impolite way. Undeterred, Vivienne jotted down the address and contact details.

Ian McAllister

Nexa Worldwide Plc

Mount Street,

Mayfair. W1K 2AP

"Mayfair. Bingo." Vivienne knew this meant *money*.

She was sitting at her makeshift desk at the dining end of her lounge which was now almost bare of furniture since Timothy had collected his personal belongings and taken far more than he had ever paid for, including the three piece cream leather suite. She was seated on an upturned box which was waiting to be filled with her favourite cook books, fiction and poetry. Unfortunately, her green leather office chair had also been taken.

She carefully wrote a covering letter in her best joined-up hand-writing on 50g ivory watermarked bonded paper. She attached to it a six year old 8 x 10 inch upper chest and face shot of a modelling photo that was used for an underwear shoot she had done some years before. Even Vivienne knew that a passport photo would not work for this high-calibre job. Going against specific instructions was a big risk, but *what the hell*, she knew her application had to stand out in the pile of hundreds she knew the Mayfair office would receive. Vivienne sealed the envelope and as an afterthought kissed it for good luck. Putting on her duffle coat, she headed for the Post Office to mail it immediately by

Recorded Delivery, keeping the receipt safely in the zip section of her purse.

Chapter Two

Mayfair – Early Summer

Richoux in Mayfair is probably the most unlikely place that Vivienne would inhabit. Situated in Audley Street and set back from Hyde Park, Park Lane and Oxford Street, people who frequented this establishment were either wealthy residents or passing tourists staying in the luxurious local six star hotels. Vivienne knew that a house around here would probably set you back a cool sixty million to start with.

A ray of early morning spring sunshine shone in through the "O" and the "H" of the gold emblem of Richoux's cafe window. It was now 9.30am on a Saturday morning, and Vivienne had been up since 6am and had made her way into London from Hampshire. She peered at her watch for the millionth time. Her designated interview slot was not until 10am and she had half an hour to kill, so a coffee seemed like a good idea.

A young, well-spoken girl of around sixteen brought the coffee over to Vivienne's table.

"Your coffee Madame." The young waitress placed the coffee carefully from the tray and onto Vivienne's table ensuring not to spill it. The poor girl appeared painfully thin, anorexic almost with a thin gold chain around her neck with a 'C' initial.

"Thank you." Vivienne smiled at the girl. Vivienne felt sorry for her. She remembered how hard she had worked as a teenager to scrape together money for things she had wanted. The girl did not fit in here; she must have travelled some distance to get to her place of work. It was true that the girl was more than ten years younger than herself, but to be called 'Madame' felt strange to Vivienne. It made her feel old and only reminded her that she was also nearly divorced, jobless and practically homeless. Vivienne shuddered.

Vivienne caught her reflection in the highly polished brass wall panelling of Richoux's interior cafe. Her thick, blonde hair was carefully smoothed down and curled under into a forties style and rested around her shoulders. Her make-up was discrete and the cool blue of her eyes were gently brushed with mascara and her full lips had just a light coating of clear gloss. Vivienne knew she had lost almost everything, but, she still had her good looks. It was all she had. It was her final trump card. In an attempt to be taken seriously, Vivienne had cut her nails short and applied a thin coating of clear nail varnish and avoided any jewellery. She pressed her lips together to bring more blood to them.

Vivienne peered down to her coffee saucer. A complimentary foil-wrapped fish with shades of aqua marine and seaweed green lay shimmering in a white and gold pottery pool made just for a chocolate treat to accompany the coffee. The tiny fish scales were outlined in sparkling gold and Vivienne ran her finger over the mould raised bumps. Vivienne stared at it for some time, turning it over in her hand. It was too perfect to unwrap and eat. *Welcome to Mayfair.* Instead, she slipped it in her pocket.

Stirring a small packet of Canderel into her coffee, Vivienne sat for a while thinking about her life up until this point. Her ex-husband, Timothy, had been an alcoholic and after a stressful day at work, would drink heavily. He would become violent, harming her often, apologising the next day. Loving him the way she did, she would forgive him. The last straw for Vivienne came when after a particularly bad bout of drinking, he had thrown a rock at her. Thankfully, Vivienne had held up her hands to protect her face, but the rock had still caused damage, breaking her hand in three places which required a cast for six weeks.

The last thing Vivienne wanted was a relationship. The idea of travel and working long hours appealed enormously. This vacancy was her means of escape. Thankfully, there had been no children from the marriage or who depended on her. Vivienne was completely free. Her situation was perfect for the job. Vivienne had weighed up her remaining options in recent weeks and if she was perfectly honest with herself, she didn't have many. The one remaining option was to move back with her parents in Berkshire. As much as she knew her parents would welcome her, Vivienne felt too old to go back there. *She had to get this job.*

Vivienne thought about the man she was going to meet, a Mr Ian McAllister, Managing Director of Nexa Worldwide. During the six, one hour telephone interviews, she had trouble deciphering his strong Scottish accent. His voice had been intimidating on the phone and very demanding. He had left no stone unturned when he had asked her about her childhood, her parents, career history, education, lifestyle, desires, personal preferences, taste of music and fashion. It did not stop there. There was also a request to apply for a Scotland Yard investigation into her background to ensure security, crime and fraud prevention. Vivienne had no idea what she was letting herself in for and was beginning to realise the enormity of the role.

Vivienne was still no more knowledgeable about her prospective employer than when she had first telephoned the office three weeks previously. It was of the utmost extreme privacy and delicacy, but he did tell Vivienne that her potential employer was a woman, semi-retired in her early sixties. It was made clear that she was highly demanding, with high expectations of her prospective employee. This was repeated several times in order to intimidate and scare off any doubtful applicants. Ian McAllister had explained only that the job required integrity, intelligent thinking, co-operation and above all flexibility. It was also made quite clear that it involved making a huge sacrifice, as it would be a 24-7 around the clock live-in role. He informed Vivienne that there would be no relations with the opposite sex during this time, little or no contact with friends and, at the very most, a daily call to family. Vivienne continued to reassure him, determined to be the one who made the final decision.

Ian McAllister was still not offering his employers' name and for some strange reason, Vivienne did not ask it. All she knew was that it would have been impolite. Vivienne's internet research had produced very little on the company except photos of the man that was due to interview her, including some brief information on multi-million pound properties available to rent in Mayfair, Chelsea, Belgravia, Geneva and Paris. The website was not serviceable or really informative, but just a means of minimum representation.

*

Vivienne was hoping that Ian McAllister would not test her basic school French. He had asked her once if she was fluent and Vivienne had replied "Un petit peu" quite convincingly. She had admitted that although she did not have a degree, she had just passed her entrance diploma to study Psychology with the Open University. She could submit monthly essays on-line with long distance study plans. Ian McAllister had commented that the degree requirement was simply to ensure that a certain type of applicant applied. He said a "hobby" would be essential during the long stints of work and months away from home, so the study element would be very suitable. He also said that his employer was in the habit of taking daily siestas, so being able to entertain oneself during these periods was essential.

*

Vivienne's upbringing had been middle class. The family home was a beautiful, large five bedroom Georgian house on the Oxfordshire/Berkshire border. She had learned to become a good listener to older, well-bred, educated bohemian friends of her parents, who lived in country estates with their dogs and horses. Vivienne did not go to private school. Her father strongly believed that if a child wanted to be educated it would work for it. He was from a poor background. He had earned himself a scholarship into grammar school and financed his own degree and was self-made.

Vivienne was bullied at school for not fitting in and friends were made from pity. Her father worked hard and was hardly at home, yet at weekends took Vivienne and her sister and mother to every single stately home in England to educate them in history, beauty and refined living.

At sixteen, Vivienne took a year of secretarial college, starting work at seventeen. Her father's motto of working hard and earning your own way pushed Vivienne to be independent.

This job offered everything to Vivienne. It was a chance to earn financial independence. But, more importantly, it was a chance to escape her recent past and to live the life of someone else and above all – to travel!

*

Vivienne felt like a fraud in her cheap black suit, even though she had dressed with careful attention earlier that morning. It was a figure hugging size twelve which made her chest look larger than she had intended it to and so she had attempted to conceal it with a pale pink dragonfly scarf. In the direct sunlight, the poor quality of the material stood out, and Vivienne had an incredible urge to run back to the safety of Hampshire suburbia.

Vivienne checked the time on her Citizen wristwatch for the twentieth time. Every minute past 9.30 had been registered in her mind. She felt nervous and began fidgeting with her mobile phone. *No messages.* She watched a couple opposite her who sat in matching rugby shirts, their Barbour jackets on the backs of their chairs. On the other side of the room, a woman in her forties sat alone in a pale blue cashmere top with a cream pearl necklace. Her backcombed hair was perfectly coiffed. She looked sad and Vivienne wondered why she was alone. Vivienne smiled in a way to acknowledge her loneliness. The woman turned up her chin and got up to browse a copy of Country Life on the magazine stand. Vivienne noticed the woman's highly tanned feet, they were the same colour as the rest of her. It was an expensive, deep, natural tan. The woman had spent months in a private villa in the south of France or St. Bart's in the Caribbean. She was wearing alligator skin slip-on mules and as she moved around the room, Vivienne could smell her beautifully refined perfume.

Outside the window and across the street, a stern looking man stepped out of 'Jeeves' the dry cleaners with an armful of plastic wrapped clothing. His simply cut black suit, crisp white shirt and black tie, suggested he must be a butler. In the window, the sun caught the crystals on the bodice of a dated raw silk ivory wedding dress. Vivienne wondered who had taken it there and so shocked were they at the price of the cleaning bill, they had not bothered to collect it. This idea made Vivienne giggle and she received a rather objectionable stare from the pale blue cashmere and pearls opposite.

That morning, Vivienne had emptied out the last of her agreed overdraft in order to pay for the train and taxi to get here. Nervously, she drummed the table with her fingertips. Vivienne received another objectionable stare from the cashmere and pearls opposite and stopped. Vivienne picked up the menu card to check the price of her coffee and nearly fainted, £4.50, plus a service charge. She could barely afford it.

Vivienne stood. Took a deep breath and smoothed down the front of her buttoned jacket, found a five pound note and wedged it under the saucer. As an afterthought, she took the chocolate fish from her pocket and put it back on the saucer just in case. Vivienne placed her mackintosh carefully over her arm to impress the cashmere and pearls, picked up her umbrella, held her head up high and left the café.

Chapter Three

Ian McAllister

Nexa Worldwide was a small office situated on Mount Street hidden amongst residential homes with a small brass plaque outside to identify itself. Vivienne pressed the intercom and the same female voice that had given the address in the first instance, told her to come inside.

Vivienne switched off her mobile and took a deep breath before entering the building. The walls were oak panelled and the floor thickly carpeted in navy blue. The receptionist sat behind a large, leather-topped mahogany desk and did not acknowledge Vivienne in any way. The recognisable intimidating feeling started to wash over Vivienne again.

"Good morning. I am Vivienne Lawrence and I am here for an interview with Ian McAllister please." Vivienne smiled. The receptionist had plain mousey hair and a navy blue suit with no make-up.

"Sit down and wait with the others." The woman almost smiled but managed to restrain herself.

There were two other girls waiting to be seen and Vivienne sat down next to them. There was a quiet acknowledgement of the three of them as they awkwardly smiled at one another. Each of them knew what they had been through to get to this very point. Vivienne wondered if any more were due to arrive or how many had already entered and left.

The two girls were called in one by one.

With grim faces, each one disappeared one after the other and left the building. Vivienne wondered whether this was from additional exhaustive questioning or simple disappointment. Hopefully the latter. The receptionist had disappeared and Vivienne sat quite alone. It was twelve o'clock. *Had they forgotten her?*

*

Ian McAllister was a tall, heavyset man with thick greying hair. He looked well fed and had red varicose veins bulging in his face from too much drinking. Although he was large, he carried his weight with ease from much practice. He had the added bonus of a beautifully made, if not oversized, custom-made superfine merino wool suit in French navy. Vivienne knew her cloth. Her mother had been a dress designer and a very good one. Vivienne had spent hours watching her sew on her machine whilst she taught Vivienne about velvets, cottons, linens, silks and wools and then about how the Americans had introduced nylon and polyester and how they had changed our way of wearing and making clothes.

Vivienne would listen in fascination as her mother told her that fabric remnants were recycled to make a fabric called 'rayon' used for high street fashion stores and supermarkets. Mother referred to this as 'tat'. She was always impeccably dressed, preferring fine quality clothes that she bought rarely to frequently purchased cheaper clothing that never lasted.

Vivienne stood up to shake Ian McAllister's hand. He looked her up and down. If he knew Vivienne was wearing 'tat', he did not show it. He gripped her hand firmly, almost painfully so and Vivienne squeezed back as hard as she could to show that she was not intimidated. Vivienne was cool and calm. She needed this job. She had not missed the CCTV cameras outside in the street, or the one in the hall pointing down to where she had been sitting patiently for two hours.

Ian McAllister appeared quite open, if not rather gruff and to the point. Vivienne knew she would have to anticipate every thought that came into his head, a skill she had mastered in her youth.

Ian McAllister took Vivienne into a side meeting room which contained a huge, highly polished mahogany table surrounded by leather chairs. The walls, like the hall, were oak panelled, except in this room they were padded in lemon silk with gold-framed oil paintings and brass picture lights. It was a boardroom of superior luxury and comfort. Another exit door was positioned at the far end of the room with a large reclining leather chair at the head of the table.

Ian McAllister pulled out a chair and sat down and offered Vivienne a seat close to his. It was an informal gesture to make her feel at ease which Vivienne appreciated.

"So tell me again Vivienne. Why do you think you are suitable for this job?" He had asked Vivienne this question about fifty times already over the telephone and Vivienne could only assume it was to ensure her answers were consistent.

"I believe I am perfect for the position Mr McAllister. I am very bright, aware of other peoples' needs, incredibly flexible, accommodating and hard-working Sir. I am fluent in conversational French. I am studying for a degree therefore I can entertain myself. I have no dependents and recently divorced so I don't want a relationship. I enjoy travelling and I am under thirty." Vivienne said in a well-spoken and confident voice.

"Good. You understand that you cannot have a relationship whilst being employed here?" He pushed.

"I can confirm that Sir." Vivienne repeated.

Ian McAllister nodded. He seemed pleased with Vivienne's answer, even though he appeared completely oblivious to the fact that he had just broken a significant employment law.

"The boss is planning to go to Geneva in a couple of weeks. She will be there for a month or two and then holiday in Paris for another month. Are you prepared to undertake this task?" he peered over his half-moon glasses, mouth open and breathing heavily. No doubt his arteries were under serious strain.

"Yes of course," Vivienne confirmed. She dare not express the fact that she had a million personal affairs to sort out if she was to fly off to Europe for three months.

Most people holidayed for one or two weeks, this was a whole new world. Vivienne had nothing else to wear and wondered how on earth she was going to present herself day in and out to a seriously wealthy female. All these problems raced through her mind in two seconds, but Vivienne smiled compliantly and maintained his gaze.

"You know what?" he slammed his hands down on the table. Vivienne made a strong attempt not to jump.

"I am going to call up to the house now. I think you are ideal for the job – it's just up to the boss now."

Vivienne watched him leave. She closed her mouth in shock. For some odd reason, Vivienne had expected to meet his boss here, if at all. Her mind raced trying to fathom all the possibilities but drawing blanks.

Vivienne waited patiently, desperately wanting to fidget from nervousness. She could feel the cold glare of a metal black CCTV camera directly above her head. The little red laser flashed on and off.

Ian McAllister stormed back into the meeting room, swinging his bulbous weight messily around the room.

"Right then. Come on young lady. It's walking distance from here."

He grabbed his mackintosh from the coat stand in the hallway, picked up his keys and some papers from the reception desk and together they walked back out into the bright sunshine.

On Audley Street they passed Richoux where Vivienne had sat anxiously three hours previously. Vivienne thought it ironic that she was now passing the café where she had sat so nervously. Another stage of this lengthy interview process loomed before Vivienne. The thought had crossed her mind whether the whole thing would be worth it.

They turned right onto Grosvenor Square. Vivienne had no idea where they were going. She felt like a lamb to the slaughter.

Ahead and to the left was a pretty enclosed park surrounded with black wrought iron railings, with mature trees and large bush roses in pinks and whites growing in their abundance.

On their right they passed the prestigious Grosvenor Hotel. Ian McAllister walked ahead in long strides, his huge feet pounding the pavement, his arms swinging backwards and forwards. Vivienne had trouble keeping up in her narrow pencil skirt and high black court shoes.

Vivienne still did not know the name of her potential employer. The intrigue was addictive and yet she felt terrified and at the mercy of this Scots man. He had drip fed Vivienne for nearly a month on a need-to-know basis.

Vivienne's mind raced. Her potential employer had to be someone famous, probably older and potentially royalty, definitely someone important enough to warrant a Scotland Yard investigation. Since this morning, everything had happened so fast. One minute she was waiting nervously amongst two other candidates who had been successful out of nearly a thousand and now, she was heading towards another prestigious address and actual home of her potential employer.

Chapter Four

Grosvenor Square

They stopped outside a huge, six storey, Georgian slab-stone town house with stone steps leading up to a large black and white tiled porch. The wide gloss black front door was flanked either side by standard bay trees. The door appeared to have no letter box or key hole. Three CCTV cameras turned and hummed above their heads flashing their red lasers.

The highly back polished door opened as if by magic. A very discrete, small Indian man peered around the door welcoming them in. Ian McAllister greeted him with warmth. They had obviously not seen each other for a while. The little man made no eye contact with Vivienne and ushered her through to follow Ian McAllister who had bounded ahead and thrown his mackintosh onto a long ornate bench in the magnificent hallway. The walls were split with a dado rail, the bottom half with mahogany panelling and the top half inlaid with antique mercury mirrors. The floor was tiled with huge cream marble slabs and covered with an elegant Persian silk and wool handmade rug.

The little man took Vivienne's coat and she followed Ian McAllister through and around to a large salon at the front of the house. In the centre of the room, a glorious arrangement of white lilies on a low Japanese black marble table dominated the room. The smell from the lilies was intoxicating and would be, in time, a significant sensory memory in Vivienne's life.

The room was beautifully furnished with cream silk sofas filling the circumference of the room in order to welcome a large number of people. In the corners of the room, four large Japanese vases inset with cream silk lampshades provided a soft glow to the room. The false light was an extravagant gesture as the sun was strong outside. On a table next to a corner sofa were four telephones. Instinctively, Vivienne avoided that seat and sat down on the other side. Ian McAllister sat on the other side of the room, quietly reading his papers.

Vivienne studied the room in more detail. The walls were covered in a pale peach, padded raw silk and edged with gold brocade. There were two huge Georgian windows to the front of the property which were adorned with peach silk swags and tails with plain muslin nets covering the zigzag security bars at the windows.

Above the marble fireplace hung a huge gold ornamental mirror and on the mantelpiece, a solid gold

French ormolu clock and matching candelabra. The clock chimed once for the half hour. It was 3.30pm.

Ian McAllister did not speak a word and carried on reading his papers. He was allowing her to take in her surroundings quietly. He had tried hard to describe to Vivienne the enormity of the position and importance of the person she was about to see. Vivienne appreciated that he allowed her to collect her thoughts prior to the final interview, although Vivienne was far from calm, her mind was reeling. To visit someone in these surroundings was one thing, but to potentially 'live' here projected a whole new light on the situation.

Vivienne's hands were tightly clasped in her lap, tensely so and realising this, Vivienne released their hold and discretely wiped them on her skirt. If Ian McAllister noticed this action, thankfully he did not show it.

Soon after, another Indian man entered the salon. He was taller and younger than the previous one. Ian McAllister greeted him. The Indian man offered Ian and Vivienne drinks to which they both declined. *Vivienne was desperate for a glass of water.*

Shortly after, the older, smaller man appeared once again. He nodded over to Ian McAllister.

"Right Vivienne. It's time for your interview. Follow Lourel here. Good luck and do not speak until you are spoken to." He did not wait for a response, but stood and Vivienne hesitated, not sure whether he was to come with her or leave the building. If Vivienne panicked momentarily, she tried not to show it. She followed the little man down the corridor.

There was moistness at her armpits against the roughness of her suit and Vivienne pulled the front of her jacket down in an attempt to separate the two. She had never been more nervous in her entire life.

Chapter Five

Her Excellency Comtesse Celeste Laisalle

Vivienne followed the little man into another inner hallway. A grand opulent staircase led to the upper and lower floors, its steps carpeted in a deep cream velvet pile. The balustrade was wide with finely carved marble which swirled around into a curl at the base of the stairs.

Ahead, the corridor widened into another reception hall and off this hall was a dining room to the left. Vivienne glimpsed the centre of a very long highly polished dining table adorned with another vase of lilies.

They continued ahead and at the rear of property, they stopped in front of a large oak panelled door where the little man knocked gently on the door. Vivienne felt lost without Ian McAllister. He had been her link up until this point. She had not really enjoyed his company, but at this moment, Vivienne wished he was still with her.

Ian McAllister had left the building and Vivienne assumed he had gone back to his office which left her feeling like Red Riding Hood visiting grandma.

"Yes." A hard, high-pitched female voice answered in a lazy, disinterested manner. Vivienne felt like running, but it was too late. She had already been swallowed and was currently being digested in the bowels of the building.

The little man opened the door into an opulently panelled office. Fitted shelves contained leather-bound books, photographs, plants and fresh rosebuds in solid silver flower decanters. To the left were four huge Georgian barred windows looking out onto an inner courtyard and garden. Vivienne walked silently into the centre of the exquisite peach silk Persian carpet in the middle of the room. She stifled a gasp as she saw who was before her. It was the very recognisable, fashion icon, charitable ambassador and role model to all women, Her Excellency Comtesse Celeste Laisalle.

The Comtesse sat quite still at her mahogany desk at the far end of the room with her head down studying her work. Vivienne knew she was about sixty-three, although in the flesh she was magnificent and could easily pass for early fifties. Her husband had been the pretender to the French throne and if the French Revolution had not taken place, the Queen of France was sitting before her.

Comtesse Laisalle was one of the richest women in the world with an estimated fortune of £800 billion. Not just wealthy through birth and marriage, but for her hugely successful worldwide property portfolio. She owned most of Mayfair, had many properties in Europe and America and probably other countries that Vivienne was not aware of. Vivienne had seen her face a thousand times in top tabloids nearly every week. They mentioned her latest property acquisition or the sale and mega profit of the same.

Her fashion sense was hot topic conversation on early morning television programmes, chat shows and evening news. Her famous, impeccably cut grey bob was copied by French women throughout France.

She was dainty, far more so in real life and, intimidating. Vivienne felt even more nervous, small and insignificant in her cheap black suit. Vivienne swallowed so loudly she was sure the older woman had heard it.

The Comtesse still did not look up. Nor did she stop what she was writing.

"Lourel, you may go." She uttered under her breath keeping her eyes on her work. The butler bent slightly from the waist down and left the room. Vivienne wondered if she should curtsey. She bit her lip feeling out of her comfort zone, unsure of the correct protocol. Ian McAllister had not warned her, so Vivienne did not. She had never heard the Comtesse speak before. The woman had never conceded to an interview on public television. She preferred pre-selected journalists with scripted questions with leading business journals or exclusive fashion magazine whose owners were friends. She had a strong melodic French accent. She spoke English with refinement and accuracy in those four little words.

Vivienne stood waiting to be spoken to. It seemed like an eternity and the silence was deafening except for a miniature carriage clock chiming four o'clock on the woman's desk. Still, this had no apparent effect on her.

Vivienne secretly scanned her eyes around the room, careful to look back at the woman every second or so, careful not to be caught peaking at the woman's belongings. There were many books with gold embossed print on padded leather spines. Vivienne was too far away to see what genre of books this incredibly famous woman was interested in reading. Vivienne was too nervous to feel excited, but she knew when she left the building she would switch on her mobile and scream down the phone to anyone who cared to listen.

To maintain her calm and focus, Vivienne peered at one of the shelves behind the Comtesse, so if the woman was to look up at her, her eyes would be facing the right direction. There were several large solid silver picture frames. One photo was taken with the Comtesse shaking hands with the French President, another with the Queen and other members of the English royal family. Another photograph was of her shaking hands with the American President.

On her desk alongside pictures of her family, was a picture taken with Brigitte Bardot sunbathing in bikinis, another with Sophia Lauren. They were old, black and white photographs and all the subjects including the Comtesse were taken when they were much younger.

Vivienne's eyes darted back to the Comtesse. She was still scribbling away. Her suit was of a fine woven woollen blush pink, and Vivienne guessed it to be Chanel. A long length of pearls with the gold Chanel emblem dangled from her neck. Her hands were bony and full of arthritis and covered with huge pink diamonds, yet she was still beautiful.

*

The Comtesse finally looked up at Vivienne over the rim of her tortoiseshell half-moon reading glasses.

"Sit down Miss…?" she said with a thick French accent and gestured with the end of her pen to one of the two armchairs in front of her desk. Vivienne sat down placing her hands flat onto her knees.

"…Lawrence. Vivienne Lawrence your Excellency," Vivienne offered.

The Comtesse continued writing, but much more slowly this time as if she were in thought as she wrote.

A hidden door to the back of the office opened about four inches and to Vivienne's surprise, a pretty little steel and gold- haired Yorkshire terrier trotted in. It immediately came towards Vivienne and jumped up onto her lap and looked up at Vivienne's face for approval. The little dog was very loving and it began to lick Vivienne's hand softly. Vivienne immediately relaxed.

"You're a lovely little dog aren't you?" Vivienne whispered through a smile.

"They say that dogs have a very good sense of character Miss Lawrence." It was a statement, not a question, so Vivienne made no reference. The woman's head had not moved a fraction and still she continued writing on her pad. She was demonstrating a sign of power and control. Vivienne felt that her personality was still under scrutiny.

The Comtesse finally laid down her pen very slowly and precisely and removed her glasses and placed them into a case nearby. Then she looked up and straight at Vivienne, the moment seemed to last an eternity and Vivienne maintained eye contact while she looked.

"Tell me Miss Lawrence. Why did you apply for this job?" the woman inquired. Her presence was intimidating, yet Vivienne was determined not to show it.

"I have many reasons why I applied Your Excellency. But the most important reason is that I feel that I have a lot to offer someone who requires personal assistance and companionship." Vivienne decided not to list the reasons as she was sure that the older woman had already been told them. Keeping her answers short seemed vitally important.

"Mmm. I suppose you were intrigued by the address of your potential employer and naturally curious. Are you curious Miss Lawrence?" the Comtesse enquired.

"Naturally your Excellency," Vivienne answered, stroking the little dog. "But not on a prying level, more on a level of what I can bring to such a high profile person as yourself."

"…and what is that Miss Lawrence. How can you know what to offer when you know nothing about me?" the Comtesse responded. *Was that a trap?*

"As I said your Excellency. I am not naturally prying, hence the reason why I have not asked why such a high profile woman as yourself would require a private companion when it appears that you have everything," Vivienne replied, trying not to sound condescending but ensuring that she sounded completely justified and matter-of-fact by her response. It was after all *The Comtesse* that was requiring a companion *not Vivienne*.

"Indeed. What makes you think I have everything Miss Lawrence?" the Comtesse enquired, raising one eyebrow at a rather strange angle.

Vivienne made an effort not to refer to high profile living that she had seen in the tabloids. "You have surrounded yourself with luxury your Excellency. You have people waiting on you. You live in the one of the most prestigious addresses in the United Kingdom after Buckingham Palace. It is a natural deduction your Excellency. I apologise if I have offended you in any way, but it is not clear to me why someone such as yourself would be interested in someone like me," Vivienne replied in a confident manner.

"You are correct Miss Lawrence. But there are still some things that money cannot buy." The woman replied. Vivienne did not comment. This woman was born into extreme wealth. She was well known to be spoilt, difficult to please and highly demanding by most people.

"Mmm. Good. You seem to be a bright young lady. Where did you study?" Vivienne was sure she knew the answer to this question.

"I studied through local authority education your Excellency and worked hard from a young age. Currently I am studying a degree with the Open University in Psychology," Vivienne replied, rather flatly. She was not going to be ashamed that she never went to University or private school. Vivienne knew that the Comtesse herself had had a governess and no formal education. Vivienne had read about this in Tatler some time ago.

"So. You are trying to improve yourself Miss Lawrence. Do you think a degree will make you a more intelligent person?" the Comtesse enquired.

"No your Excellency, education cannot make you a more intelligent person. I believe intelligence is either present or not. Education only supplies information that can be used to the persons' benefit, to broaden their knowledge on a chosen subject or to achieve their career goal in life."

"Mmmm. Clever answer. You are an interesting character Miss Lawrence. What about charitable concerns. Do you involve yourself in those?" she questioned.

"I have done. Yes, your Excellency. I have raised money for charities including Aspire and Cancer Research," Vivienne replied honestly.

"Excellent, they are two very worthwhile charities. I myself support many worthwhile charities which you will no doubt become involved with over time."

"What do you think of me Miss Lawrence?" the Comtesse enquired, changing tactic.

Vivienne was taken aback by this question. Honesty would not be appropriate here, and a lie detectable by this world-wise older woman.

"You seem to be a very intelligent, experienced woman your Excellency, someone whom I might be able to learn a lot from whilst providing a professional service to." Vivienne held her head up.

"Clever girl. You certainly know how to conduct yourself Miss Lawrence. Mmm. Good." She gave a half-smile at this point and her features began to soften somewhat.

"Do you know who I am?" she questioned. *Are you joking?*

"Yes your Excellency. You are The Comtesse Celeste Laisalle," Vivienne responded as politely as she could muster.

The Comtesse stood then and leant across the table and offered Vivienne her right hand to shake. Her left hand stayed her swaying necklace. Her full height without seeing her shoes must have been about five foot five, she appeared much shorter in real life. Vivienne half-stood then, trying not to stand to her full height so as not to overpower the older woman and shook her warm hand gently. Vivienne then curtsied and the little dog jumped from her lap and trotted back out of the room.

"My main home is here in England, but I also have homes in Paris, Geneva, New York to name but a few. Do you like to travel Miss Lawrence?" she asked.

"Indeed I do your Excellency. Ah, should I call you Comtesse?" Vivienne enquired.

"Yes. That is fine. To unfamiliar people you would address me as Her Excellency Comtesse Laisalle, and for those that I am familiar with you may address me as Comtesse," she informed rather helpfully.

"What does your father do for a living Miss Lawrence?" she was now leaning back in her reclining leather chair playing with her pearls.

"My father has his own business resource management company Comtesse," Vivienne informed.

"Interesting. So your father is a businessman Miss Lawrence. Good. What about your mother. What does your mother do?" she enquired.

"My mother stayed mainly at home and raised my sister and I, but when she was younger, she was a dress designer Comtesse."

"Ah. A dress designer, interesting," she said unconvincingly. The Comtesse eyed Vivienne's clothes then, obviously unimpressed.

"...and where do you shop for clothes Miss Lawrence?" Vivienne wanted to say dress boutiques or Max Mara Sport or French Connection. It was obvious she was not wearing designer clothing, so she was not going to lie.

"Mainstream stores Comtesse and if I require something more elaborate, I make it myself," Vivienne hoped the woman would be impressed that at least Vivienne was able to solve her financial dilemma with her own skills.

"Excellent. Very good. What do you think of my suit Miss Lawrence?" The Comtesse maintained vigilant eye contact.

"The fabric is a pure wool blend and hand woven and hand dyed Comtesse. I believe it is also custom made as it fits extremely well. I would guess that it is Chanel due to the cut, the colour and type of fabric they are known to use."

"My my. You are a surprising person Miss Lawrence. I shall have to keep a careful eye on you I think."

They were interrupted by the ring of one of the telephones on the Comtesse's desk.

"Excuse me one moment." The woman removed a pearl encrusted clip-on earring and answered the telephone.

"Yes?" she looked over to Vivienne. "Yes. Thank you." She hung up. Thirty seconds later, the phone rang again.

"Thank you Ian. La Tante Claire. Good idea. You have the paperwork ready?" She had waited whilst he spoke on the other end and then hung up the phone. Vivienne noticed that she had not asked him of his plans for tonight and it was clear that most people around here were on a 24 hour on-call service.

"So. You will accompany Mr McAllister and myself to a restaurant tonight. Let's say you should be back here for 7.30pm."

"Thank you Comtesse. I look forward to it." The woman stood as if to close the meeting and Vivienne immediately stood and curtseyed.

"You do not need to curtsey to me anymore Miss Lawrence. Thank you," the Comtesse informed.

"Thank you Comtesse." Vivienne left the room.

Five minutes later Vivienne was back out on the street and took a deep breath of fresh cool air. Vivienne looked at her watch – she was in the middle of Mayfair and had only two hours to change into evening wear and return for her final interview.

Chapter Six

The confidentiality agreement

Vivienne arrived back at Grosvenor Square at half-past seven and was shown into the salon by the little Indian once more. Earlier, she had taken a taxi to Harrods. It was the only place she knew where to go as her mother, her sister and herself had frequented it many times when she was growing up.

Using her emergency credit card, she bought a cocktail dress, shoes and a pair of shiny skin tone holdups. In the ladies room, she had swiftly changed and reapplied lipstick and touched up her hair, all in view of the attendant clerk who watched her with amusement.

The Comtesse was sitting in the corner sofa and to her side on the table was a glass of pink champagne in a champagne flute.

"Hello Miss Lawrence. Welcome back. Come, have some champagne." The Comtesse gestured to a seat to her right and Vivienne sat down. It was exactly the same chair Vivienne had sat in earlier in the day.

The little dog came running in and jumped up onto Vivienne's lap and she stroked her soft hair lovingly, the little dog licked Vivienne's hand appreciatively.

"Her name is Esther. It seems she has a new friend now," The Comtesse said plainly. The little butler arrived with a silver tray with a glass of pink champagne balancing upon it and offered it to Vivienne.

"Ah, no thank you. Just water please," Vivienne replied. This was another catch, she was sure. Vivienne was not an alcoholic and was not going to lose the chance of a job for a glass of champagne.

The little man looked in a surprised fashion at the Comtesse and then spoke to Vivienne for the first time.

"Would that be sparkling or still please?" he asked in a melodic Indian accent, tilting his head from side to side.

"Sparkling please," Vivienne replied, feeling very uncomfortable that this little old man would have to go somewhere a long way away to bring back a glass of sparkling water for her. There appeared to be no drinks cabinet in the room.

The Comtesse had gone quite quiet. She had placed her champagne glass back down on the table. It was not long before she picked up the handset on one of the telephones on the table.

"Pastor? Bring the car round. Immediately." The older woman retorted.

There followed a deafening silence. Vivienne dared not to speak until the older woman spoke first. Vivienne did not know what had just happened other than that somehow she felt that she had just blown it. She began to backtrack over what she had said. Maybe she should have accepted the champagne. *Golden rule number one. Never drink at an interview or an important meeting.* It was too late. Vivienne could not change her mind, so she sat there waiting for the inevitable end. It would come, she was sure of it. The little man came back and informed the Comtesse that the car had arrived. The water forgotten, the older woman rose from her seat and Vivienne rose too.

"Come Miss Lawrence, time for dinner." It was an order. Vivienne let out an invisibly long breath that she had been holding for some minutes.

In the hall, the little man dressed the Comtesse with her evening coat and the younger Indian man presented Vivienne with her mackintosh, open, ready to help her into it. It was not an evening coat, and uncomfortably, Vivienne took the coat and instead placed it over her arm. The Harrods bag which now contained the clothes she had worn earlier in the day had been placed in the coat cupboard by the younger butler.

The sun had long gone and the evening night was drawing in. On the curb, a large black shiny Mercedes was waiting with a CL1 private number plate. Another, far older Indian man with a black cap, black suit and black leather driving gloves stood waiting, holding the rear door closest to the pavement for the Comtesse. Vivienne had no idea what to do, so she stood there on the pavement waiting. For the first time Vivienne truly felt like a companion, just like Joan Fontaine in the film *Rebecca.* The man ushered Vivienne around to the other side of the car and opened the door for her. Sitting down onto the wide leather seats, Vivienne had a massive urge to touch the door to close it, but contained herself when the chauffeur undertook this task for her. Noticing Vivienne's discomfort, he smiled a secret smile.

The car appeared custom-made and was fitted with four telephone handsets, just as Vivienne had seen in the salon at the Grosvenor Square mansion.

*

La Tante Claire is a very exclusive member's only restaurant in Mayfair. In fact, like many exclusive clubs or restaurants, it is very difficult to determine them as they are so carefully concealed. La Tante Claire is one of them with whitewashed woodwork and white blinds and a pair of the usual topiary standards outside the entrance

– there is nothing else to give away the fact that it could be a restaurant. Even for famous celebrities, two weeks' notice for a table was customary.

The Comtesse did not have a pre-booked table, slipping two fifty pound notes into the maître d's hand via a handshake, a table was suddenly whisked out, quickly laid and two chairs pulled up. Mick Jagger sat opposite with a female companion. He looked up at Vivienne, wondering who she was as Vivienne accompanied the famous Comtesse Laisalle.

After they were seated, Ian McAllister arrived in a fluster and apologised to the Comtesse profusely for being late. A third chair and place setting had materialised as if from nowhere. His attitude towards the Comtesse was buoyant, respectful and flattering.

The Comtesse excused herself and rose from the table to go to the ladies room and Ian McAllister spoke down to Vivienne, in a whispered manner.

"Now look Vivienne." It was the first time he had called her by her first name.

"Lourel told me you refused a glass of champagne at the house and asked for water. That will not do. Her Excellency the Comtesse has to have a companion with whom she can share a bottle of wine when I am not around. Don't tell me you're teetotal." He slapped his forehead as if to punish himself that during all those telephone interviews he had failed to ask one of the most important questions.

"No, not at all Mr McAllister, I am just trying to do the right thing," Vivienne replied, eager to please.

"Oh, thank God for that. So you do drink then?" he reaffirmed eagerly.

"Yes. I do, occasionally," Vivienne responded carefully, thinking this another test.

"Good. Good. Great. Okay. Waiter? Bring the sommelier please."

The sommelier arrived promptly wearing a little silver tasting cup hanging around his neck on a long belcher link chain. An intricate, solid silver grape brooch sat proudly in place on his lapel. Vivienne noticed the wine list at the back of the menu card that she had been given. Prices for wine started at £70 and went up to £10,000. Ian McAllister made his choice, nonchalantly. The sommelier puffed out his chest and bowed deeply to Ian McAllister and departed promptly.

After a while, the sommelier returned and began to hop around their table filling the air with extravagant gestures. He held the bottle at an angle and showed it to Ian McAllister who nodded. On Ian McAllister's approval the sommelier began to dust down the old-looking bottle with swift, sharp exaggerated movements.

Very carefully and silently the cork was removed and the eccentric man waved it in front of his nose. It twitched and his eyebrows drew together. He then continued to pour a little of the red liquid into his silver tasting cup. He swirled the liquid in a clockwise direction at high speed, so much so Vivienne thought she was going to be coated in the stuff.

The whole of his nose then entered the cup as he took a deafeningly deep sniff and then slurped a sip of wine. Finally, he threw his head back and drew his mouth into an oblong shape. He raised his eyes to heaven which Vivienne assumed to be a good thing. She stifled a strong urge to burst into laughter by biting the inside of her cheek.

At last, the sommelier was ready to pour a sample into Ian McAllister's glass to confirm its suitability. It seemed as if he was reluctant to give us any of this expensive liquid which he coveted like his own private stash.

Ian McAllister appeared deadly serious as he took a sip and finally gave consent that he was happy with the wine. The sommelier nodded in agreement and proceeded to decant the whole bottle into a large bulbous glass decanter, pouring it through a delicate tiny silver sieve. He did not present it to either of us. Our wine glasses still empty. Vivienne took a sip of her water.

"It is extremely important Vivienne that you learn the very basics about wine. You will become an expert in vintages very rapidly as the Comtesse only drinks the very best. The obvious things to look out for are mould, corking, temperature, acidity and sediment. All of these things are an issue when dealing with vintage bottles. In time you will learn the difference between a good wine, a very good wine and an excellent wine.

You will never have a bad wine with the Comtesse unless you are in residence and you should ask for this to be replaced immediately, even before the Comtesse takes her first sip. Believe me, this will save a lot of grief towards the butlers and yourself.

In a restaurant, a sommelier will do this work for you and if you have chosen a vintage wine that the sommelier thinks is off, you will of course not be charged and a similar choice will be made on your behalf. Sometimes, it might be necessary to tip a sommelier if this happens as you should appreciate their honesty.

You can recognise a sommelier quite easily. They stand apart from waiters in their dress and also by the fact that they only serve wines. But, most importantly, they will always be wearing a set of solid silver grapes on their left lapel which is presented following qualification on a four year sommeliers course. It is an honourable degree and they are hired exclusively for this role in only the best of restaurants. Always, always ask for the sommelier. Never, ever trust a waiter with a vintage wine."

*

Ian McAllister took a breath and then a sip of sparkling water from his water glass. He placed his elbows on the table and made an arch with his arms, his fingers touching at the precipice.

"Corking can happen with any wine with a cork bottle stop, hence why nowadays, screw tops, rubber and plastic tops are used. There is a lot of controversy over the use of these modern methods and some wineries still only use cork as it is the preferred method by wine connoisseurs.

So. Corking occurs when the cork has either started to deteriorate with age or when the wine has started to acidize and break down the cork. Alternatively and more frequently, when the cork is opened badly and bits are left in the wine – hence why you never allow a waiter to open your wine, as an older cork is more likely to crumble when removed and has to be withdrawn with great delicacy and by an experienced sommelier."

He took another sip of water, glancing at the resting wine in its new home. He touched the glass decanter lovingly.

"It is absolutely necessary to allow a decanted bottle of wine to rest in order to allow any sediment to reach the bottom of the decanter. Then, just a small amount of wine should be poured at a time and very slowly, this is to ensure that little or preferably no sediment is passed to the wine glass." He touched the bottom of the decanter with his forefinger.

"You see – there is sediment building now. The sommelier used a wine sieve, but still some has escaped. The older the wine, potentially the more sediment it will carry, hence why we don't really drink wines older than about forty years."

Vivienne stared at the glass decanter in amazement. She wished she had a pen and paper.

"If the weather is cold, the wine will need to be brought to room temperature more quickly in a restaurant once it has been decanted. A tea light candle under a wine cradle is sometimes used. Hence why a red wine glass is bulbous in shape, in order to warm up the wine faster in the palm of your hand, similar to a brandy glass. In contrast, a white wine glass is narrower to maintain its cool temperature and should be held by its stem to avoid contact with body heat.

Heat brings out the flavour of red wine, but it can also deteriorate the wine very quickly, hence why it is imperative that the wine is stored in a cool place, on its side to ensure the cork remains wet. If the bottle is stored upright, the cork becomes dry and will start to crack, allowing air into the bottle and mould to grow, making the wine undrinkable."

"Moulding occurs when the cork is so old that it has become porous allowing air to get into the bottle. And if you think that this is all there is to remember, you are wrong. All this is when you have correctly chosen the right vintage." He took his arms down and crossed them as he leaned towards Vivienne. He gestured in a manner to which he was going to tell her a great secret.

"You see. Even if you get a well-known makers mark, you can still have a poor harvest. No rain. Too much rain. Too much sun. Not enough sun. All these factors determine whether a vintage is going to be successful or not. Hence why many famous makers discount their wines hugely and sell them, but they just don't taste as good! Why is that? It's because they had a poor year – saving the better vintages for higher mark-up in years to come or for personal use."

"So the vintage is the year is it made?" Vivienne asked.

"Yes. Yes Vivienne. Look, don't worry. It will come to you in time. I knew nothing about wine before I met the Comtesse – she is a mine of information. If you care to, you can learn a lot from her. In the meantime, I have devised a little list and had my secretary print it for you. It tells you all the years over the past forty with the makers mark and the good vintage years. The years printed in red are those that you should avoid. Keep this with you like a Bible and refer to it when you order wine for the Comtesse, but discretely Vivienne. Always absolute discretion where the Comtesse is concerned. She likes to think that all those who serve her are the best. Never, ever tell her you don't know something. Tell her you will find out."

"Thank you." Vivienne was very grateful and she took the list and glancing at it, placed it quickly into her handbag.

*

As the Comtesse returned to the table Vivienne could not help but notice the other diners who were making a contrived effort not to appear star-struck as she passed.

"Ah Comtesse. We are having a Romañee Comti '86". Ian McAllister stood up and pulled out the Comtesse's chair.

"Oh super, an excellent choice Ian. I didn't know there were any '86's left! OH I am pleased" She clutched her hands in sheer delight, just like a child might if she was told that Father Christmas was on his way.

*

As the evening progressed and wine was drunk, Vivienne became a little more relaxed. The Comtesse asked Vivienne about her childhood and where she grew up. Vivienne talked about her time in South Africa when the family went to live there for her father's business. The Comtesse laughed merrily at a funny anecdote. Vivienne began to find Ian McAllister charming and it was clear that the Comtesse was very fond of him. He talked about his wife and children and he seemed to be very happily married.

The Comtesse gave Ian McAllister full credit for the choice of wine as if he had made it himself. Ian McAllister seemed to be an expert in entertaining the Comtesse and flattery was not wasted on her.

"Is that a Chanel suit Celeste or Vivienne Westwood?" It was the first time Vivienne had heard the Comtesse's first name spoken.

"Oh come on Ian. Are we really going to talk about what I am wearing? But you are right. It is Vivienne Westwood. I thought I would wear it in honour of our Vivienne here." She leant towards Vivienne and tapped her on the hand. It was the first physical contact the Comtesse had made towards Vivienne. Vivienne felt honoured.

The Comtesse seemed pleased that someone had noticed her beautiful clothing and at the same time sent a compliment Vivienne's way. The older woman was a marvel to watch as she entertained with ease.

"So Vivienne. How do you like Mayfair? Is it what you expected?" inquired Ian McAllister. The Comtesse turned her attention to Vivienne.

Vivienne crossed her legs. Celeste watched Vivienne intently and glanced at her legs as the opening of Vivienne's suit dress fell away. Vivienne readjusted her clothing quickly and the Comtesse continued to wait for her response. Vivienne had noticed the Comtesse's unusual interest in her bare thigh.

"I honestly did not know what to expect Sir, but it is very charming. Thank you," Vivienne replied politely. The Comtesse and Ian McAllister passed a knowing look between them and they all talked for an hour or so more, working their way through a tasting menu. Ian McAllister and the Comtesse talked a little on a new business opportunity he was working on whilst he drank. Vivienne became relaxed and enjoyed listening to his Scottish accent curl around the business terminology. Another bottle was ordered.

Vivienne did not normally drink red wine, but its fruity velvety thickness was amazing on her amateur taste buds. She avoided the sediment at the bottom of her glass which was not missed by the Comtesse.

The sommelier came to change their glasses in preparation for the next bottle. The food was light but exquisite and every mouthful melted in Vivienne's mouth. For the first time in her life, Vivienne felt like she was being seduced by food and wine.

Vivienne did not want to finish her plates, ensuring that she left something as a sign of politeness. It was noted. Nothing went amiss. Ian McAllister and the Comtesse seemed to be able to communicate telepathically.

The meal was over and Ian McAllister reached into his briefcase for some paperwork. The Comtesse eyed him carefully. They seemed to have a common understanding about what was to happen next. He shuffled the papers in an attempt to order them and failed. He cleared his throat.

"It is necessary for you to sign some papers Vivienne before you agree to accept this position. It is quite normal that a job of this calibre comes with some secrecy elements due to the high level of media interest in the Comtesse's private and business affairs. Do you understand?" he was deadly serious now.

"Yes. I understand," Vivienne said.

"I have here what is known as a Confidentiality Agreement between Comtesse Laisalle and yourself." He continued.

"...and I am here to witness its signing. I have to make it quite clear that if you do not sign this agreement, then the position you are being offered by the Comtesse will cease at this point. Do you understand?" Ian McAllister repeated.

"Yes. I understand." Vivienne understood very clearly. *Sign the papers or no job.*

"I suggest you take a few minutes Vivienne to read through the papers and ask me if there is anything you don't understand. Please, do not sign anything you are not clear about" his straight body language made Vivienne sit up straight. The restaurant was still busy with customers, yet their table was silent. Mick Jagger and his female guest were long gone. Vivienne glanced down at the paperwork.

This *Confidentiality Agreement* is between *Her Excellency Comtesse Celeste Laisalle* and *Miss Vivienne Lawrence*.

The Agreement is made on the date of the last signature below between

1. *Her Excellency Comtesse Celeste Laisalle (Disclosing Party) and Miss Vivienne Lawrence (the Receiving Party).*

2. *This confidentiality agreement and any amendments; any information disclosed by or on behalf of the Disclosing Party to the Receiving Party during the Term that at the time of the disclosure is confidential in nature or may reasonably be considered to be commercially sensitive and which relates to the business or private affairs of the Disclosing Party. Effective Date: (a space to be completed and signed).*

3. *Obligations in relation to Confidential Information. To withhold information or to prevent information being leaked to or supplied to any media source. To restrain and to protect the high profitability of the nature of the business and private affairs herewith.*

4. *Term of Agreement*

This Agreement comes into force on the Effective Date and continues until death of Comtesse Laisalle or both parties.

5. *Third Party Disclosure*

No party may assign, transfer, sub-contract or in any other manner make over to a third party the benefit or burden of this Agreement. So, Vivienne couldn't speak to her mother, her best friend – no one.

"I am here just to witness the signing of the paperwork and ensure it is handed back to our lawyer's office. Of course, you will receive a copy for your own records." Ian McAllister spoke in a very low voice over the table, the fingers of his hands locked together.

A waiter came and asked if they wanted coffee. The Comtesse declined and Ian McAllister and Vivienne followed suit. Instead, the Comtesse took a gold encrusted filigree enamelled pen from her handbag and handed it to Vivienne.

"I hope you will sign it Vivienne dear. It is my wish."

Vivienne took the pen and held it between her fingers. The pen represented the Comtesse so well. She was a woman who could buy anything she wanted. *Apparently even people.*

Vivienne looked over to the other diners – she felt they were all staring at her, but each table was engaged in their own conversation. She looked back down at the papers and after reading their contents, signed. If the Comtesse had held a tight breath in her mouth, she let it out and smiled.

"Welcome aboard Vivienne. Let's celebrate." Ian McAllister called over a waiter and ordered a magnum of champagne.

Chapter Seven

Remuneration

"I do so love a Louis Federer Rosé champagne, don't you Vivienne?" the Comtesse questioned. Vivienne couldn't care a fig, but had always loved champagne but never been able to afford anything beyond a Bollinger.

"It's delicious Comtesse. Thank you," Vivienne replied truthfully.

The Comtesse was now calling her Vivienne and her manner was much more relaxed. Vivienne was still very much unsure how to brooch the subject of the role in hand and of course the salary. Now that Ian McAllister had been dropped back at the office in Mount Street, she felt that these finer details were not going to concern The Comtesse whatsoever. Back at the mansion house on Grosvenor Square, the Comtesse and Vivienne talked for what seemed like hours and yet they still had not talked about money. It seemed rude to even mention it. Vivienne managed to convince the Comtesse quite well that she was there purely for the pleasure of her company, although Vivienne was still in awe of this famous woman. There was no doubt that the Comtesse was entertaining and interesting, but never in all her life had Vivienne met such a narcissistic and self-appraising woman. Vivienne was still not sure whether she liked her or not and constantly reminded herself that this was not relevant. This was a job.

"Why don't I show you your private quarters?" The Comtesse suggested, getting up from the settee and leaving the room without waiting to see if Vivienne would follow.

The two walked down the long corridor that Vivienne had passed earlier in the day. The grand staircase loomed in all its grandeur. Vivienne followed obediently. She felt like the Comtesse's little dog, Esther, as she descended the staircase.

"In this house, the best rooms are in the basement in my opinion." The Comtesse swished her black organza skirt as she placed her foot onto the first thickly carpeted step.

The steps were shallow and wide and Vivienne felt as if she was gliding down to the floor below. At the bottom there was a huge television room with fitted mahogany units. There were photo frames, travel books and small personal items of silver, bronze and crystal. A huge white leather sofa wrapped around the centre of the room facing the television. To the right corner, a swing door went through to a marble kitchen and staff quarters. To the other, access to an impressive wooden conservatory filled with palm trees, orange, lemon and olive trees on a marble stone floor lit up with red night-time warming lights.

"This is your private television room. No one will use this room except you." The Comtesse declared.

Vivienne followed the Comtesse, glancing back at her own television room with interest. Through an archway, there were two further doors. The Comtesse opened the nearest door.

"These are your private quarters, and through here is your bathroom." Vivienne followed the Comtesse and entered a large bedroom with an en-suite bathroom. The Comtesse waved her arm lavishly around the room. The bathroom was stunning in white marble with gold plated goldfish taps. A large rectangle mirror was surrounded by lightbulbs which were glaringly bright, perfect for applying makeup. All around were fitted cupboards for supplies and a heated towel rail filled with fluffy white towels.

"...and this is your bedroom and dressing room." The room contained a pair of bedside tables and elaborate, hand-painted silk lamps. There was a small double queen size bed and the coverlet was made of a soft pink silk and cotton mix jacquard, cross stitched with gold thread. The same luxurious material covered the padded walls and padded, weighted curtains. A flat screen television was placed on the wall. A fitted mirror wardrobe filled one side of the room. A large modern dressing table in white marble surrounded with more Hollywood lightbulbs. By the window, a dark pink raw silk sofa looked out to the inside of the beautiful conservatory.

"Now I will show you my rooms." She walked out and Vivienne followed appraisingly.

They left Vivienne's quarters and were back in the inner-hallway and entered the other door. From here another inner hallway with two more doors.

The Comtesse pointed to one door. "Through there is access to a gym, Jacuzzi and a swimming pool. It is heated, so don't worry," she commented and continued walking.

Further down the corridor the Comtesse opened the last door. "These are my rooms."

They entered a huge, magnificent room, with mahogany wall panelling on one side with double-fronted fitted wardrobes. There was a TV cupboard that, to the touch of a button produced a large flat screen television. To the nearside wall, a long chest of drawers, containing many pills and potions and the customary four telephones in a glossy cream standing in a line with their unusual push buttons in different colours.

A huge emperor size bed with four pillows and an abundance of cushions dominated the room. There were two giant night stands situated on either side of the bed with shiny brass lamp lights on long arm hinges fitted to the silk draped walls for night time reading. Vivienne was beginning to learn that the Comtesse not only enjoyed luxury but that practicality had to play an important role in her home decor.

Vivienne glanced at the Comtesse's nightstand, a pile of books and a pair of reading glasses were left haphazardly as if the occupant of the room was to shortly return.

On the far side of the room was a dining table with two beautiful rattan mahogany chairs. Further on, a picture window adorned with silk swags and tails gave access to the conservatory and back garden.

The en-suite bathroom was incredible and equalled the size of her bedroom. A marble, oval sunken bath dominated the centre of the room. Leaning over its side, a gold leaf mermaid sat with her molten hair flowing down to her waist. She held a lobster pot on her left hip from which water filled the bath. Orchids, strelitzia's and bonsai's surrounded the tub giving it an appearance of a tropical haven.

On the other side of the bathroom was a walk-in shower wet room, toilet and bidet, surrounded by mirrored cabinets. The older woman took Vivienne through to the dressing room which had another access door to the Comtesse's bedroom. The dressing room was the size of five double bedrooms fitted with wall to wall mirrored wardrobes. In the centre, a large circular pouf in white raw silk was placed conveniently for the Comtesse to sit comfortably whilst she dressed.

"I have a new gadget that I am very proud of, would you like to see it?" the Comtesse half opened one of the mirrored doors and Vivienne had no idea what the older woman was going to show her.

"...ah yes. Yes, of course," Vivienne stammered.

"It's my automatic clothing closet. Look. You press this button and the whole thing whizzes round." The Comtesse was a little exited as she showed Vivienne her highly prized piece of engineering just for her clothes. The Comtesse pressed a button and immediately the machine whirred and clothes started to circle round. Each item turned to face her and stop before it turned back and carried on behind the mysterious cavern behind the hidden mirrors. There must have been over twenty thousand dresses and suits contained in the wardrobe. It was extreme wealth, more than Vivienne could have ever have imagined.

"Isn't it fun?" the Comtesse declared turning up the speed and her dresses whizzed past, each in a colour coded section of their own.

To the far end of the Comtesse's dressing room was a dressing table that looked like it had just been on the set of a Cleopatra movie. Its large inverted gold scallop shell hugged an equally large oval dressing table which was draped in white gold silk. Upon the glass top a selection of solid gold embossed hair brushes, combs and atomisers of perfume and a large dust puff of silken talcum powder in a crystal hand-cut dish.

Vivienne imagined the media would have a field day photographing these private rooms and she could see that the Comtesse was happy to finally show off her private domain.

"How about a splash in the Jacuzzi with another bottle of champagne? Would you like that?" she did not enquire, it was an order. The older woman thrived on showing off her house to Vivienne and as they entered the pool room, Vivienne had to admit she was impressed. The pool must have been fifty feet long and twenty-five feet wide with mermaids surrounding the pool. They were exotic marble figures with different coloured hair in liquid enamel and with each one had different sized breasts, some really large and some almost flat. Vivienne thought it odd, yet extremely eccentric and the room offered yet another glimpse into the inner mind of the Comtesse. To the ceiling, the basement windows were just below street level and Vivienne could see the shine from the street lamps above. The inner bowels of the house reminded her of a maze hidden below floor level. Vivienne had never imagined that the houses on Grosvenor Square could hold such a magical underworld.

Into another room, there was a fully-equipped gym and a running machine and to another side was a sunken Jacuzzi flanked by mirrors all around with parlour palms on either side. A fridge was situated in a fitted alcove between the gym and the Jacuzzi where the Comtesse retrieved a bottle of Cristal from the many that were shelved there alongside small bottles of water and four chilled champagne flutes. She retrieved two glasses and a bottle of champagne and popped it herself, laughing as the top shot off and banged the ceiling.

"Oops – there she goes!" The Comtesse stumbled backwards and giggled like a young school girl.

"Through there are some swimming costumes if you want to choose one – feel free."

Vivienne turned and went into a dressing area where she chose a small black full costume with a deep V in the front. It was slightly small and her breasts bulged uncomfortably. The Comtesse was already in the Jacuzzi with her Westwood dress flung over one of the running machines and a few smaller items of clothing on the floor in front of the Jacuzzi. Her shoulders were tanned and bare.

"You don't mind if I skinny dip do you?" she enquired as she passed Vivienne a full champagne flute. The warmth of the Jacuzzi and the bubbles of the champagne were a delight and immediately Vivienne felt even more relaxed. This time they talked about travel which Vivienne could relate to and they laughed as they compared private jets to "pigeon carrier" flight companies which the Comtesse admitted she had never had the joy of experiencing and Vivienne told her she must.

"...it's like having someone sitting in your lap that you don't know!..."

The older woman laughed and looked at Vivienne in a strange longing way which made Vivienne feel a little uncomfortable. Vivienne turned her head away.

The Comtesse took Vivienne's face and cupped it in the palms of her hands.

"So beautiful. Do you know how beautiful you are?" she breathed in a heady manner. They both had had much to drink.

"Thank you Comtesse," Vivienne responded, suddenly sober.

"If you decided to employ me Comtesse, I would need a salary to pay my own way in life." Vivienne finally found the courage to spit it out.

"Ah….money. It always comes back to that. Yes, you are right. I had quite forgotten. Well, for a live-in role such as this I would be prepared to offer you an annual salary of £500,000 and a car if you want one – I assume you can drive?."

"Yes, I can drive. Thank you Comtesse. You are very generous."

"I can get Ian to arrange everything." The Comtesse finished her glass. She had closed the discussion.

*

Back in Vivienne's private rooms where she had retired to re-dress, Vivienne stared at herself in the bathroom mirror. Her knuckles paled against the sides of the basin.

"I shall not be overwhelmed…"

The Comtesse had called the chauffeur to drive Vivienne back to Hampshire. It was agreed that Vivienne would return on Monday morning. Ian McAllister would set up a payroll for £500,000 per annum, plus expenses, plus clothing allowance of £100,000 per year. Payroll details would be set up on Monday with Ian McAllister and the first monthly instalment of £50,000 less tax would be in Vivienne's account by the end of the week. Expenses would be claimed back on a monthly basis through the head office on Mount Street. A car would be delivered, brand new, ordered for Vivienne and chosen by her for her return from Paris in three months.

The money Vivienne was being offered was crazy. It answered all her prayers and solved all the problems that lay around her and meant she could finally wash her hands of Timothy, her old house and enable her to literally walk into a new life.

Chapter Eight

Moving in

Vivienne arrived on the Monday morning with her small suitcase of toiletries and a suit carrier with the two outfits that she had worn at the interviews. She wore a simple navy blue dress suit that she had bought from Phase Eight on the Sunday, maxing out another credit card.

She was immediately greeted by Esther who ran and jumped up into her arms. The Comtesse was sitting having her morning coffee watching the international news channel. The TV had been pulled out to the centre of the room from behind a hidden Japanese screen. A newswoman was blabbing away in French.

"Mind the wires darling," The Comtesse called out, getting up to give Vivienne a hug. Gone was the woman from the first day. She appeared to be very happy and excited to see Vivienne.

"Have a coffee darling while I finish the news and then we will talk." She pushed the red button on the house phone and without talking to anyone, the younger butler came rushing in.

"Coffee for Miss Lawrence please Matos." He nodded and left. This was the first time Vivienne had heard the Comtesse use *please* to one of her staff and she imagined it must be the happiness that had brought this display of politeness. Vivienne liked this side of the Comtesse. It was her doppelganger that in time, Vivienne learned to detest.

Vivienne had finished her Blue Mountain coffee. It was delicious and the best coffee she had ever tasted in her life. Vivienne later found out that the Comtesse would have professional tea and coffee tasters arrive from Fortnum & Mason to offer her the finest choice blends.

"Now dear. I would like you to go down and fetch my handbag for me, I have left it in my bedroom. Inside is seven thousand pounds in a white envelope. Bring the handbag up to me will you?" The television had been returned to its home and the older woman sat and waited for Vivienne to return with the handbag.

Esther followed Vivienne, fast at her heels as she went down to the basement floor below. Through the conservatory Vivienne noticed the garden. She had not seen it before as it had been dark when she had been there the night before. A grand veranda containing gigantic stone urns filled with lilac trees in mauve and white dominated the front edge. The heart- shaped heavy heads of the lilacs were magnificent under the bright light of the late spring day. It was a little early for lilac trees, but Vivienne suspected that the enclosed courtyard garden and the warmth of central London brought the blooms into flourish. The garden was beautifully inviting and the grass so lush and green. Its uniform stripes mowed in perfect lines from the veranda to the formal garden at the rear.

Vivienne found the Comtesse's handbag on one of the rattan chairs. Inside was the envelope. She brought it straight back.

The Comtesse took the handbag and opened the envelope and counted the money. She seemed satisfied.

"Good girl. You did not touch a penny. There is ten thousand here. You could have taken three and brought me seven. You passed my most important test. Many have failed it. Now, I will give you cash this time because I assume you need it, the rest will be in your bank account by the end of week when you have supplied Ian with your bank details." The Comtesse handed the envelope to Vivienne.

"Now. Go onto the Kings Road and buy some nice suits dear. Good quality ones, something for the day and something for the evening. Not too dressy mind. Look professional." The older woman leaned closer and

Vivienne had the feeling she wanted to tell her something sensitive.

"Also…you know, you are rather tall dear, so I would prefer it if you bought some flat shoes to wear all the time. You will also require jogging shoes. Every day I walk out very early and I want you to accompany me, alright darling?" she leant over to Vivienne then and kissed her sweetly on the cheek. Vivienne was dismissed.

Out onto the street Vivienne walked, with no direction in mind. She had no idea where she was going. Soon she passed Claridges and crossed the road and went into Bally where she bought a lovely pair of tan peep-toe shoes with a low heel.

Falling by chance onto the Kings Road, Vivienne went into Marc Marc and bought a crisp white linen jacket with a soft silk beige double layer silk dress. She bought another linen casual sleeveless jacket for walking and had just spent £3,500. Vivienne soon realised that the Kings Road was best left for the super-rich and instead she hailed a cab for Harrods, the only place she knew.

Vivienne entered Harrods by the west door and headed straight for Perfumery. She bought a large bottle of "*essence – eau de musc*" by Narciso Rodriguez following a convincing advertisement in a copy of *Tatler*, a past edition which Vivienne had found in her private television room.

In the shoe room, Vivienne bought a lovely pair of black satin Stuart Weitzman shoes with a little heel plus a small handbag to match. In ladieswear, she bought several suits from MaxMara, including a gorgeous navy blue dress with a white banded top and jacket to match. Vivienne decided she needed a handbag to match her new tan Bally shoes and headed back to the ground floor where she bought a tan Chloe handbag for £1150. It had taken Vivienne just two hours to spend £10,000. The same amount she had spent on her first car.

In excitement, Vivienne called her mother. She dug around in her handbag for her mobile and speed-dialled the number.

"Hello?" Vivienne instantly recognised her mother's quiet voice.

"Hi Mum. It's Vivienne." Vivienne's mother insisted on calling her Vivienne, unlike her friends who always called her 'Viv'. Vivienne's mother interrupted anyone who dared to call her anything else.

"I'm just calling to tell you that I have a new job." Vivienne started, unsure how she was going to describe this one.

"Oh great love. What are you doing?" she asked sounding naturally curious.

"Ah, um. I am working in Mayfair for a French aristocrat. Very wealthy. Old. Nice. It's a live-in job, so I don't need to worry about where I'm going to live."

"Mayfair. Oh. Good. The money should be good then?" Vivienne's mother asked innocently.

"Very good mum. I will be able to sort Timothy out and all my finances, so you won't need to worry about me," Vivienne said reassuringly.

"Sounds good love. Can I have the address and phone number and the name of the person you are working for?" Vivienne's mother was not a fool and cared deeply for her youngest child. She was not about to let her live anywhere without knowing where and with whom. Vivienne gave her the number, name and address. There was a silence.

"What is she like?" she sounded dumbfounded.

"Well. She is exactly as she appears in the tabloids. She is nice, generous and kind. I will be well looked after. I am flying to Geneva in Switzerland soon, that's really why I'm calling. Just want you to know where I'll be and that I will be there for some time. I will call you when I arrive. Is dad okay?"

"Yes dad is fine. Don't worry about us. Just take care of yourself. Call me when you arrive in Geneva."

"Love you mum. Bye." Vivienne was reluctant to hang up the phone, it could be a long time before she spoke to her mum or dad again, let alone see them. Vivienne felt bad about telling her mother that she was in Harrods and had just spent ten thousand pounds. She would only worry. Leaving Harrods, Vivienne took a taxi amongst those waiting outside for shoppers and headed back to Grosvenor Square.

Chapter Nine

Matos

One evening as Vivienne was getting ready for dinner, she closed the thick padded silk curtains in her bedroom. As always, she ensured they overlapped as she always did. Esther was laying on her bed, licking herself and glancing at Vivienne from time to time to ensure she was still there. The Comtesse had informed Vivienne that they were due to dine out at La Gavroche in Mayfair and Vivienne was in a good mood. The first few weeks had been successful. The Comtesse seemed happy with Vivienne and Vivienne with her. Their friendship was building steadily and so was the Comtesse's trust in Vivienne which Vivienne was sure must be difficult for someone with her kind of wealth and standing.

Vivienne's own personal issues had all been resolved quickly thanks to a healthy bank account. The bank manager himself had called Vivienne's mobile to inform her that it was not safe for her to leave a large sum of money in her current account, and that he advised transferring most of it to a more secure account that would earn interest. Vivienne was not used to this kind of attention. She was entering a new world of wealth. On a far smaller scale than the Comtesse to be sure, but still, her life was looking bright and her future seemed secure.

At La Gavroche, the Comtesse praised Vivienne's sense of taste and style in clothes. She seemed in a very jovial mood and Vivienne enjoyed the Comtesse's company more and more. She had chosen to sit at a booth table where the two could sit side by side. The Comtesse chatted merrily with the Maitre'd who she seemed to know well and introduced Vivienne to him with pride.

"Now listen here Tom. This is my new companion Vivienne. Her eyes are my eyes and her choice is mine. Do you understand Tom?" she continued to chatter on without waiting for a reply and Vivienne felt a little embarrassed at this poor waiter who had to suck up to her for his bread and butter.

Every now and then Celeste patted Vivienne on the knee, the hand or forearm and occasionally kissed Vivienne on the cheek when appraising her hair or carefully applied makeup.

Vivienne felt like a pet and was not used to such attention and as every day passed, the Comtesse became more and more tactile towards Vivienne. This did not particularly bother Vivienne, she was just happy that her own company was pleasing this older woman who paid her to accompany her around the clock. It was an easy and enjoyable job and Vivienne felt grateful and very lucky. Although, Vivienne had no space or free time to herself. This was the sacrifice. Vivienne knew she was building towards a secure future, laying the foundations of her new life. Secretly, Vivienne knew that one day she would be able to leave the Comtesse and finance her own life. These small sacrifices for a few years seemed worth it for a future that would be financially secure for her.

*

Accompanying the Comtesse was unique. It was all very new to Vivienne and strange. Everywhere they went people knew the Comtesse, everyone. People in the street, doormen, cleaning staff, reception staff, waiting staff, everyone. Of course she was famous. Vivienne had known of her also. But accompanying someone so famous was an odd experience. Vivienne became part of it and within a couple of months was remembered also wherever they went as Miss Vivienne or Miss Lawrence. People began to bow or curtsey to Vivienne as they would to the Comtesse. Vivienne's photo's appeared in media photos with the Comtesse with the same catchphrase... "who is she?"

Soon the media wanted to know all about Vivienne and called her for interviews which she kindly refused and instead they attempted to rake cobwebs from an empty closet. Instead, they would ask where she had shopped, what designer she preferred and where and what she preferred to eat.

Vivienne could no longer visit Harrods without the manager rushing down to greet her as soon as word got round that Miss Lawrence was in the building. Life suddenly was not her own.

Vivienne knew she had earned the role. The interviews had been strenuous and she had been determined, but still she was receiving the same privileges as a princess which she did not feel comfortable with. The Comtesse and Vivienne's worlds were miles apart. Vivienne was a commoner. When she entered the Comtesse's world, she became a Princess within minutes and Vivienne would stare at herself in the mirror and see a more beautiful self, thinner, healthier, better fed, better exercised, well dressed and at times she did not recognise herself. Vivienne's family and friends were in awe of her and her job. They marvelled at the places she went and began to wait on every message or call that could tell them who she had seen or who she had spent time with, usually a famous royal or a President.

But, Vivienne was lonely. She missed her ex-husband. She missed her old house. She missed a takeaway and a movie. She missed simple things like going to the cinema or watching a girly flick with a girlfriend over a cheap bottle of wine.

She missed a fried egg on the weekend or a takeaway from her local Chinese. It was the little things she missed the most.

Ironically, within a few short months, Vivienne found it difficult to blend into normal society.

*

One day, Vivienne found herself queuing half an hour to pay for a tube of hair shampoo. In frustration, she decided to leave it and sent Matos out to buy it instead. Vivienne's life was changing. Vivienne was changing. She was evolving and she did not know whether she liked herself the better for it. Time became valuable. Vivienne was only allowed six hours off to sleep in a twenty-four hour day, plus two hours in the afternoon whilst the Comtesse took her siesta. Seven days a week work with only a week off a year to visit her family and friends. It was a tough work schedule. The rich were happy to pay but expected faithful service around the clock.

Vivienne rarely had the luxury of spending a few hours shopping for clothes or visiting the hair dresser.

The Comtesse preferred to have designers visit the house so she knew where Vivienne was. She was a very controlling woman and in time Vivienne truly felt she was owned by her.

Vivienne's days often mirrored the Comtesse's unless the Comtesse had an important business meeting which was too confidential for Vivienne's ears. Vivienne would escape during these long meetings and go for a coffee or a walk in the park or call her mother away from the tapped phones. Such was the Comtesse's insecurity and paranoia that Vivienne would hear the secondary click of a raised handset somewhere else in the house when Vivienne received a call.

The Comtesse's schedule was rigorous and Vivienne followed suit. Up at 4am, breakfast, 4.30am power walk. 5.30 shower. 9am meetings or the news reports and financials. 10am progress meeting on her property investments, 11am charitable meetings, 12pm lunch, 1-2pm siesta, 3pm news reports, 4pm fax reports of financials, 5pm tea, newspaper reports, 6pm shower and change, 7pm aperitif, 8pm dine. 11pm night cap at Grosvenor Square or wherever. 12pm bed. Then the day would start all over again. And so it went on. Month in month out.

*

One evening Vivienne returned to her bedroom and undressed and put on her night gown. She was tired and her movements were slow and clumsy. As usual, Esther had followed Vivienne into her bedroom and had already curled up to sleep at the bottom of Vivienne's bed, occasionally peering over at Vivienne with her little adorable puppy eyes.

Vivienne heard a shuffle and was not sure where it had come from. Esther's head raised up and her ears pricked up to listen more attentively. Vivienne was quite still. There. Another shuffle and then a creaking noise. Vivienne turned to face the window. Esther jumped down off the bed and onto the sofa, poking her head between the parted curtains. Parted curtains. Vivienne had left them closed and wrapped over as she always did. Matos. He had entered her room as was customary, to turn down her bed and switch on the bedside lamps and he must have parted the curtains. Esther was growling at the window. Vivienne knew that on the other side was the conservatory.

Vivienne put on her dressing gown and left the room. She entered the conservatory and noticed a cane garden sofa backed up against her bedroom window for whose benefit she was not sure, but on this occasion, it was Matos. He had turned her bed down and meddled with her curtains and watched her undress. Vivienne felt sick. She shuddered and returned to her bedroom and reminded herself that from this point on, she would ensure her curtains were always closed. She also knew that if she mentioned it to the Comtesse, Matos would be sacked and sent back to Goa the next day and all of his family would suffer the silly incident. Vivienne decided to drop the matter, but keep a close eye on Matos from now on.

The next morning Vivienne accompanied the Comtesse for her ritual 5am walk around Hyde Park with Matos who was used as a bodyguard during those morning rituals. Vivienne did not say good morning to Matos on this occasion and avoided eye contact. Whether this change of behaviour was noticed in Matos or not, Vivienne did not care. Dutifully, Matos followed five paces behind the Comtesse and Vivienne as he always did and Vivienne took her mind away from the incident of the previous night. She would let him off this time, but if something happened again, or worse, she would have to report him to the Comtesse. Vivienne hoped that her ignorance of Matos would be enough to demonstrate that she was aware of him the night before. Instead, Vivienne increased the speed of the power walk with the Comtesse maintaining level pegging. Vivienne was always impressed at how fit the Comtesse was and enjoyed challenging the Comtesse to increase her distances daily. The two kept up their pace right around the lake and back to Grosvenor Square.

Vivienne returned to her quarters and had a shower before falling back into bed. She would rise again at 8.00am to read the Comtesse her morning papers at 9am.

Chapter Ten

Quai Wilson, Geneva – summer

On the fourth week of Vivienne's employment and in mid-July, the Comtesse and Vivienne arrived in Geneva airport by private jet. It was the first time Vivienne had ever travelled by private aeroplane and it was beyond her expectations. An airport official entered the aircraft to check passports, including Lourel's – the Comtesse's private butler, and the hired staff that managed the aircraft. Matos and Pastor had gone on ahead by road two days earlier to make ready the Comtesse's apartment and to provide a means of transport for Her Excellency. Pastor was obediently waiting on the runway in the Comtesse's Mercedes ready to collect the three of them. Lourel carried the Comtesse's briefcase. Vivienne's suitcases had been taken by road and had already been unpacked and prepared by Matos who was now waiting patiently at the apartment with refreshments prepared.

The Comtesse talked about Geneva and how much she loved its clean air. How they would walk around the lake and water spout every morning as she did in Mayfair to maintain her slim figure. Vivienne had noticed that she herself was losing weight dramatically. The Comtesse's personal chef was an excellent cook and was ordered not to use any fat in any of his preparations. The Comtesse's diet consisted of smoked wild salmon, beluga caviar, fresh salads without dressings, turbot, seabass, sea bream or lemon sole and nothing else. Vivienne ate what the Comtesse ate and asked no questions. She also drank what the Comtesse drank which became Vivienne's saviour during the long hours of work. Vivienne never had one hangover. The quality of the wine was such that it never warranted one. The stress of the job, the long hours, a fish only diet and early morning walks were all factors to Vivienne's weight loss which had plummeted to 50kg.

*

The heat and clean air hit Vivienne immediately as she alighted the aircraft and sat next to the Comtesse on the cool leather back seat of the air-conditioned Mercedes. After forty minutes they arrived at the Geneva Lake and the famous water spout and drove round onto Quai Wilson where the Comtesse had her private apartments. The law in Switzerland is that cars must turn off their engines at red lights to ensure air quality is maintained and it is true, the air is supremely fresh.

The Comtesse had a magnificent third floor apartment overlooking the lake and positioned next door to The President Wilson Hotel. There was a magnificent stone archway at the front of the property with a double hand-carved solid oak communal front door. The shared hallway was palatial and cool. A beautiful fresh breeze blew in from the lake. A stone spiral staircase with iron work balustrade lead to the upper floors. Alternatively, a small lift for three persons. Vivienne was welcomed to the Comtesse's apartment by Matos, who swept open the heavy oak front door to greet them. The floor and hallway of the apartment were dazzled by a huge glass lantern hanging from the ceiling. The walls were dramatic and wallpapered in an opulent magenta pink. The floor was tiled in a chequered black and white marble. To the left was a library in oak panelling with a view that people would pay thousands for. A desk was positioned by the window with a computer, telephones and a photocopier and this is where Vivienne would work most days. There was a kitchen off to the right with staff quarters off from there. Along the hallway and off to the left overlooking the bay was the dining room which had a magnificent glass oval dining table, a breakfast sideboard and above it a Japanese hand-painted country scene depicted on a very old scroll. The window opened up over the lake and the view was breath-taking. In every room, the fresh air blew in from the lake and the sun glinted to make everything look romantic and exotic. A double door opened from the dining room into the grand salon which was the most magnificent of all the rooms. This opulent room had dramatic long wooden picture windows which gave a majestic view of the water spout on Lake Geneva. At one end of the room were two cream silk sofas facing each other with a coffee table and a large antique bureaux. At the lake end of the room and over a beautiful dark pink Persian carpet, was a shiny black grand piano, two further lounge chairs and a telescope. At each bay window seat, cream silk cushions were placed in order to sit and watch the world go by. Vivienne had never seen such a magnificent room.

The grand salon had another exit which led back onto the hallway with three en-suite bedrooms.

The first room was Vivienne's and she preferred this room to the one in Grosvenor Square. The walls were covered in a beautiful padded mauve silk dupion with small hand sewn embroidered silk flowers. Vivienne touched the thick opulent material appreciating its fine quality. The bedspread was in the same material as was a huge kidney-shaped dressing table with a grand ornate mirror. A canopy of white muslin adorned the mirror in a draped fashion. Vivienne felt like a Princess seated there. The view from Vivienne's bedroom window was of the city which at night lit up with buzzing lights. Up an elevated step was her bathroom which was surrounded in white marble. From the bathroom was an enormous dressing room with large long mirrored doors.

Along the corridor, another double en-suite which was a guest room and then, further on, the Comtesse's private rooms.

At the entrance to the Comtesse's rooms was an inner hallway with a display of her favourite fresh white lilies presented in a bulbous clear glass bowl. There were two doors from this little hallway. One to the left where the Comtesse slept and another to the right which gave access to her dressing-room. Another, additional inner door from her bedroom serviced the entrance to this dressing room.

The Comtesse's Genoise bedroom was even more luxurious than the one in Mayfair. The first thing that hit Vivienne was the breeze as all the windows were wide open with an inviting window seat giving the same views as the salon and the library. An elegant set of two chairs graced a fine small dining table with white lilies for the Comtesse's private in-room dining. To the left, one wall was covered in mirrors and the other, a huge Emperor bed with an opulent headboard and bedside tables. The Comtesse's en-suite bathroom, shower room, sauna and Jacuzzi were decorated in soft pastels and gold.

The Comtesse had common complaints of a woman of her age. Her circulation would be the worse issue. Her legs would require rubbing down with oil and she would wait patiently for Vivienne to come at six o'clock following her bath to rub them down with her exclusively prescribed oils. Following this she would insist that Vivienne accompany her into the sauna where she would demonstrate that rubbing the skin to get the sweat flowing was essential.

"To help you manage the heat darling. Sweat in here and you won't sweat outside." Vivienne found that the older woman was true to her word.

The Comtesse was excessively generous and loved to spoil Vivienne. On Mont Blanc Avenue she bought Vivienne a Cartier ruby and diamond ring that cost her £40,000. Although it was stunning, she had maintained control by choosing it for Vivienne and bargaining the price down by ten thousand. She insisted that Vivienne should have a full black mink diamond coat even though it was boiling outside.

"One only buys mink in summer darling; it is twice the price in winter." Vivienne spent the rest of the afternoon thinking how many little minks had had to die in order to cover her back. She was sure a faux would have been just as nice. The Comtesse had had it sent by air to Mayfair and to her furriers where they would remove the lining and freeze the skin to ensure it did not get musty in any way. Vivienne had tried her hardest to persuade the Comtesse not to buy it – insisting for the first time in her employment. The Comtesse had not relented. Vivienne felt that it was more about wanting

Vivienne to appear more suitably dressed in her company than any personal preference that Vivienne had. Although Vivienne had the last word and indeed never wore the garment again.

Vivienne became the Comtesse's walking Barbie. The Comtesse picked out clothes for Vivienne, had her hair re-styled, shorter and into her neck and back away from her face with a high fringe. Vivienne relented, but she felt it made her look far older than her late twenties, another tactic to make the Comtesse more comfortable with her presence. She ordered masculine cut suits in different pinstripes with shirts and ties and Vivienne thought this rather odd – but could see that the Comtesse loved it and for an easy life, Vivienne went along with it. Vivienne became the tipper. Where ever they went, Vivienne would be given a pile of notes and the Comtesse insisted that Vivienne tip the table attendants and the sommelier on arrival. The Comtesse was famous for her generosity everywhere she went and received the accreditation that she had so carefully invested in.

"There is no use tipping after you've had your meal and after poor service. Ensure you always tip at the beginning Vivienne to ensure the best service and best food possible darling." To Vivienne this made great sense and she adopted this train of thought from that moment onwards.

Celeste was a mine of information. She knew everything about everything and everyone.

"You know Vivienne – I know that famous Princess was murdered?" she would whisper.

"I have friends in very high places and especially in Paris, Vivienne. A woman was seen standing on the bridge who saw the Princess walk from her car crash and she was subsequently murdered. The undercover paparazzi dragged the poor Princess back to her car and pummelled her to almost death. When this did not work, they ensured that the ambulance travelled to the furthest hospital to ensure the Princess was too late to receive the surgical assistance required to save her life." Vivienne was shocked; the Comtesse knew things about people in the media. As soon as someone famous came on the television, she would tell Vivienne all about their lives, their tax evasions, their homes in Switzerland, where their money was invested, all about their secret love lives and different families in different parts of the world.

One weekend, Ian McAllister flew in from Scotland where he was on vacation with his family. Everyone took vacation when the Comtesse was out of the country except her personal staff and excluding her Mayfair chef who would take a month off work to see his family in Goa. Lourel and Matos would also take their month off in turn, but only when it suited the Comtesse.

"Remember who you are…" Ian McAllister said to Vivienne one evening over dinner when Celeste had gone to the powder room.

Vivienne constantly wondered what Ian McAllister meant by this. She thought he implied that she was no-one, insignificant and replaceable. If Vivienne had accumulated wealth, jewels and luxury clothes, it would not be enough to turn *a nobody* into *a somebody* and she should remember her place.

Chapter Eleven

An unwanted approach

Vivienne supposed that one day the real reason for her employment might come about. Something wasn't straight about the Comtesse. There did seem to be a hidden agenda. There had been several occasions when Vivienne had felt compromised one way or another by the older woman. The first time was when her skirt fell away at the first dinner, the second in the Jacuzzi, the third on arrival in Geneva and whilst in the sauna when they were quite alone.

One night after returning from evening dinner at the Hotel Richmond, Vivienne had a quick shower and washed her hair before joining the Comtesse in her private rooms to watch television together as was customary.

Vivienne wore her thick white towelling robe and the Comtesse wore her silk negligee as she always did when relaxing in her private rooms.

Vivienne would relax on the far side of the Comtesse's bed and together they would watch National Geographic or news reels whilst sipping wine from a chilled ice bucket. Vivienne had always felt very comfortable with this arrangement until now.

The Comtesse was bored of watching television and decided she wanted to massage Vivienne's shoulders to demonstrate how it ought to be administered onto herself. Vivienne was used to massaging the Comtesse's legs and thought this was perfectly acceptable and acquiesced to the Comtesse's slightly unusual demand. After all, the Comtesse was a woman. What harm could it do?

Vivienne's dressing robe was removed and the Comtesse deftly massaged Vivienne explaining her moves as she worked her back. Vivienne was not uncomfortable with the Comtesse's hands on her and thankfully the Comtesse avoided private areas. The Comtesse's energy though became more intense. Vivienne could feel the Comtesse's emotions through her hands as she worked Vivienne's back using her thumbs to identify each vertebrae and release the tension there. She was a good teacher, although as time progressed, the Comtesse's movements became slower and increasingly sensuous.

"I have never really ever been in love you know Vivienne." She spoke finally.

"Not even with my dear Gaston. No. That was an arranged marriage. I loved him, of course I did. Like a brother. Well, we were married thirty-seven years." This revelation shocked Vivienne and instantly she felt sorry for the older woman and thought that even wealth could not bring happiness or perhaps allow you to marry whom you desired.

"I am sorry to hear that your Excellency." Although Vivienne was apprehensive, she was relaxed and the scent of the lavender in the oil had softened her muscles as well as her senses.

"I don't think you need to call me that anymore Vivienne dear. You may call me Celeste from now on, but in private only." Her hands had stopped working.

"Thank you...Celeste." Her name felt strange on Vivienne's tongue. She felt it was insolent, but the older woman had asked of it and in most cases it appeared to be the nature of the job for Vivienne to comply.

"Have you ever slept with a woman before Vivienne?" Celeste said, quietly. Vivienne was face down and this question came as a shock to her. *Where was this leading?*

"Never. I think I prefer men." Vivienne was sure to add that she preferred men to end any potential further suggestion.

"Ah yes. Well, we all love men, but with a woman you can have a far more intense experience. Women are witches you know? All women." This was a statement. Vivienne would not question it.

Celeste turned Vivienne around then and leant down to kiss her on the mouth. From instinct, Vivienne quickly got up and rushed into Celeste's bathroom and locked the door. The situation had finally gotten out of hand. Vivienne finally knew what Celeste was after and she would never become that. Her body and soul were not for sale. Vivienne had never been with a woman before, let alone one Celeste's age. The massage Vivienne could cope with, the woman was lonely, but this was too much.

Vivienne peered at herself in Celeste's luxurious bathroom mirror. She was now faced with a choice. She truly hoped that Celeste would not force her to make one. The rejection might be too much for Celeste, her ego and fragility was too sensitive to be able to cope with such a rebuff. Their friendship might even now be compromised.

Vivienne slammed down her fist on the enamel sink in anger. Disappointment raged through her. She would have to leave Celeste and go home.

Vivienne had been in Celeste's bathroom for some time. When she returned to Celeste's bedroom, Celeste was watching television. Quietly, Vivienne returned to her usual place on the other side of the bed. It was clear that Celeste was not happy and finally she excused Vivienne for the rest of the evening. That night Vivienne slept restlessly.

*

The next morning Lourel knocked loudly on Vivienne's bedroom door at 4.30am to remind her it was time to get up for the Comtesse's 5am walk.

Celeste was relentless that morning, power walking with an aggressive swing in her arms and legs. Both Matos and Vivienne had trouble keeping up with her. She was in a foul mood. The rest of the day continued as it had started. Everyone was deadly quiet in order not to upset the woman. During lunch, Vivienne sneezed at the dining table. Vivienne felt she had caught a chill from the fresh morning fresh and running to keep up with Celeste.

"Do you have a cold Vivienne?" she was sharp and slightly uncaring. It was the first time she had spoken all day.

"No Comtesse. Just an itchy throat." Vivienne did not dare to call her Celeste after the night before and especially not in front of the house staff as she had requested.

"Good. Because if you have a cold, I don't want you around me. Do you hear? I don't want to be laid up for a week in bed ill," she stated flatly.

*

The next day Celeste left the house very early and had left a message with Matos that she would be out all day and afternoon and that Vivienne should entertain herself. This was a clear message of disapproval.

Not too worried, Vivienne decided to go out for a long walk. For the first time in weeks she felt free and exhilarated.

Vivienne needed time to think. To think about what she would do if Celeste dismissed her. Or more importantly, what she would do if the older woman tried to seduce Vivienne again. Vivienne took the path by the lakeside and sat down on the concrete breach wall and allowed the sun to warm her face.

Celeste had been generous, but still Vivienne had no idea that the woman wanted more. Vivienne was not a lesbian and could never envisage becoming one. She could not believe that the woman she had known for so long through the media and tabloids was actually a lesbian. Celeste's marriage had been a sham. She had children and was a grandmother. She had carried this secret all her life. Vivienne felt sorry for her.

The more Vivienne thought about it, the more her mind reeled. She knew that she would have to draw a compromise with the Comtesse somehow or she would have to leave. When Celeste was in such a foul mood, it was impossible to want to remain in her company, no matter how much the privileges.

Vivienne could not give Celeste what she wanted and she battled how she was going to tell the spoilt older woman this.

Chapter Twelve

Valentin – the roller-blader

The sun glistened across the lake and with each wave that rippled back to the shore, silver ribbons of sea spray blew in the air. Far beyond the waves and out into the lake, the stillness was magical, the surface of the lake offering a mirage on the horizon. White yachts glistened on its still surface – too many to count. The sunlight became a backlight to each white sail. The sight was almost ethereal.

Tourists and residents were escaping the heat of the midday sun. Restaurants were at their busiest as people escaped the hottest part of the day. The promenade was almost bare, no one risking sunburn.

The sun beat down onto Vivienne's head and she was glad she had brought her huge white hat to shade her pale face. The hem of her long white dress swayed in the breeze of the splash. A large steamer passed and the tourists waved as they headed out towards Lausanne.

Vivienne headed on beyond where the lakeside path stopped and allowed access for more serious walkers into the parkland of the United Nations Head Office, a grand stone building with huge long windows with balustrades, and an immaculately mowed front lawn with large cedar trees. Down by the water's edge, the path wound left and right through firs and rhododendron trees. The path wove further and further away from the lakeside and into another park of the United Nations Building beside the lake.

A passing roller-blader whizzed past with long tanned legs, gliding in and out as he expertly sashayed across the smooth paving slabs. He almost knocked Vivienne down. Ahead, his arms swayed back and forth in a balancing movement. His grace and energy portrayed the epitome of male youth in all its glory. After spending weeks and weeks in the company of Celeste and her staff, his presence and youthfulness was a breath of fresh air. The young man wore headphones over a pair of funky Ray bands and he turned and waved. Vivienne was not sure if that was a *"hi"* or a *"sorry."* Maybe a bit of both.

He turned at the end of the pavement where it joined the additional park and headed back towards Vivienne. Just a second before colliding into her, he glided expertly around her, running his fingers through the swaying muslin of Vivienne's white billowing skirt.

Vivienne found him refreshingly annoying, yet exhilarating at the same time and she did not know whether to continue walking or to turn around and see if he would be coming back. Finally, Vivienne turned and he was far down the promenade, swinging his arms and stretching his legs at a speed that should only be allowed on the road. Luckily there was no one around except herself and eventually Vivienne turned back and carried on walking.

Often, Vivienne thought of Esther and how much she would have loved it here. She missed her. Celeste did not want Vivienne to arrange a pet Passport for the little dog, but Vivienne made a secret promise to her out loud as she stopped to stare out at the lake, that she would bring her here with her the next time she came. Vivienne knew that Rosa, Celeste's housekeeper would take care of her, but still Vivienne worried about the little dog knowing full well that she would be unhappy without her new mistress. Vivienne felt that it was jealousy that drove Celeste not to consent to a Pet Passport for little Esther.

The sun was getting too hot and Vivienne searched for a shady spot under some trees to escape the boiling heat. She removed her hat and laid back on the grass, crossing her arms over her head so that her hands fell behind her.

She was almost asleep when something made her start with a tap to her arm.

"Hey...what are you doing?" Vivienne sat up alarmed and saw it was the young roller-blader standing in the sun just outside the perimeter of her shaded space.

"Ah...mademoiselle. Do not be afraid. I just wanted to talk to you. You are English no?" he gave Vivienne a cheeky smile and his perfectly aligned white teeth glistened in the sunlight. His muscly slim arms glistened with sweat from exercise. The muscles at his knees bulged from expert practice at his choice of sport. It was difficult not to marvel at his perfect male form.

"My name is Valentin. You know – like the love day. You say, Saint Valentine's Day, no?" he spoke in a thick sexy French accent. If Vivienne was miffed at him disturbing her, this was soon gone.

"Yes that's right." Vivienne was not sure whether it was a good idea to be making conversation with this young man and so she put on her dark sunglasses so she could hide her thoughts.

"May I ask your name?" Valentin shifted weight to his other leg, one foot vertical in order to press his rubber stop down into the pavement.

"It's Vivienne," Vivienne said slightly unsure whether it was safe to be giving out her name, especially as she had just arrived in Geneva. Vivienne looked about to see if she could see any butlers or house staff lurking.

"You seem nervous Miss Vivienne. May I sit with you?" He asked this, but sat anyway into her shaded

115

patch. He nodded and a silly grin appeared on his face. He spread his legs out in front of him and into the sunshine.

Vivienne felt awkward. He was a very young man and obviously trying his luck on what he thought was a tourist. They sat for a while looking out at the lake. His silence made Vivienne smile inside as she could feel his lack of experience in chatting up women. Vivienne felt like she was teasing him now.

"So. You here on holiday?" Valentin enquired, another flash of his beautiful teeth. His cheeks highly set and a smile that reached his ears.

"No. I am working," Vivienne replied rather stupidly as she was obviously sunbathing. She especially did not want to get into a conversation about what work she did.

"Oh yes? You work in the town?" Valentin was trying hard.

"Ah no. I have a place I stay at the Quai. It is complicated, I would rather not talk about it." Vivienne looked in the other direction to reaffirm that she had closed that particular line of conversation.

"It's okay. We don't have to talk...what is it you English say...ah...shop!" he smiled again and nodded. He seemed very pleased with his English.

He made Vivienne laugh then and he seemed pleased that he had managed to make her relax.

Vivienne glanced at her watch and she realised that it was time to get back to the house, whether the Comtesse was back or not.

"Sorry Valentin. It's time for me to get back to work." Vivienne tapped her wristwatch assuming that he might not understand her. She rose to get up but Valentin was there before her, helping Vivienne to stand. The super-fit and gorgeous roller-blader reached for Vivienne's hat on the grass and brushing it down, passed it to her.

"I understand. Me also." He nodded. "Maybe I see you again down by the lake?" he enquired, waiting keenly for more information.

"Maybe. Nice to meet you. Bye." Vivienne walked off and turned to wave, but Valentin had zoomed off ahead. His blades spread and his legs performed an acrobatic twirl in an attempt to impress her. Vivienne laughed and waved. The roller-blader was swift to leave then, as quickly as he had arrived, his young pride not allowing him to be left hanging.

Chapter Thirteen

Pierre and Delphine Laisalle

The Comtesse returned later that evening and seemed a little more relaxed and no longer angry. Vivienne thought that she had been missed a little and Celeste had had time to soften her resolve. They dined in peace in the dining room and thankfully Celeste did not ask about Vivienne's day. Vivienne was happier than usual as she thought about her fun encounter with the roller-blader. She had her own little secret that she did not want to share with anyone, let alone Celeste. It was wonderful to have her own secret from Celeste. The older woman would be infuriated if she knew. Vivienne had never met such a jealous person.

"Tomorrow, we are going to my son's house in La Colonie up in the mountains. It is very beautiful up there, the air is crystal clear and the views are spectacular. You will like it, I am sure," she informed Vivienne.

"Thank you Celeste. I look forward to it." Vivienne sounded convincing because she meant it. She was happy that they would not have to spend the day with each other alone as the period of awkward silences was still not over. Vivienne shivered. She had decided not to mention the incident of the previous evening and to avoid the subject in the hope that it never happened again. To her benefit, Vivienne knew that Celeste liked her and knew she enjoyed her company. After all, Vivienne was hired to entertain Celeste and accompany her wherever she pleased, but that was all. The Confidentiality Agreement had not mentioned that Vivienne would have to act in any way that would compromise her honour. Vivienne would have to stand her ground and make it clear that that was all she was prepared to give Celeste.

"Are you cold Vivienne? I will get Matos to bring you a shawl." She lifted her head to gesture towards Matos who was standing behind Vivienne, waiting for any need she might have. Lourel stood behind Celeste, his eyes averted into the air.

"No Comtesse, thank you. I am fine," Vivienne reassured her. Celeste seemed satisfied although eyed Vivienne with an inquisitive sideways glance that appeared to be untrusting. The poor woman was always in doubt of herself and it was clear, that she was deeply insecure of her aging self. She was a woman who was definitely not comfortable in her own skin and Vivienne felt pity for her.

*

The next morning was very foggy and this only denoted that the day ahead would be hotter than ever. The small party headed up to the La Colonie at around eleven, passing through the city of Geneva and taking a side road sign posted *La Colonie,* onto a steep mountain road. The road wound up and up through lush fir trees. The air became clearer and Pastor turned off the air conditioning and opened all the windows for us to take in the fresh air.

"My son Pierre runs our Geneva office and he does an excellent job of it. His wife Delphine is an antique collector and runs an interior design company." Celeste sniffed and turned away.

Vivienne immediately got the impression that Celeste did not think much of this Delphine for whatever reason. Vivienne looked forward to deciphering this for herself and at the pleasing discomfort of Celeste's mannerisms.

They passed many houses and Celeste pointed out whose house was whose, including Tina Turner's. To Vivienne's continual amazement, the entrance to the

Laisalle Villa was opposite Tina's house and slightly higher up in a more exclusive position. It was flanked by electric security gates and a guard standing with an arm gun hoistered into his black leather hip belt standing next to a little guard house. He recognised the private numbers plates of Celeste's car, peered through the open tinted windows and waved us through.

"The higher the property, the better the view." Celeste declared proudly. The drive wound round and round and climbed higher still. The steep walls of rock were flanked with shrubs and low lying firs. The driveway at the front of the villa wound round a fountain of a mermaid and the ground became flat, the gravel on the driveway crunching and sounding our arrival. We were exactly on top of the mountain.

"Over there is Mont Blanc. You can see it, but the top is in the clouds. Sometimes, you can see the very top on a clear day." Vivienne peered over to the mountain opposite where a snow-capped peak hid between the clouds. The main entrance to the two storey villa was very grand and yet simple – its architecture inviting for a summer's day and striped yellow and white awnings protecting all the windows from the sun. The whole ambience had a holiday feel. There were hibiscus everywhere in deep rich reds and pinks. Palm trees swept down to the other side of the villa where Vivienne could imagine the views to be incredible.

A rather short, stocky man came out of the villa to greet them. He appeared typically French, dressed in white, shorter than average, in pants and white espadrilles. His attitude was casual and so was his dress. There was an air of quiet authority about him and extreme confidence that only comes from people who are as rich as Celeste. Vivienne assumed that this of course was Pierre, Celeste's son. "Welcome, welcome. Good day mummy. You must be Vivienne. Welcome to our home. Make yourself at home, please..." he gestured to the party to enter.

The villa itself was modern Spanish architecture in a hacienda style. The huge expanse of floor was tiled in small, red clay tiles and the walls were a refined mustard yellow. Upon them, huge slabs of what appeared to be sections from the tomb of an Egyptian pyramid, hung majestically from the high walls on an open gallery landing. Steps down took them through to a huge salon with large linen-covered sofas filling the room around a big glass, rectangular coffee table upon which another object d'art of a stone nude stood in all its glory in the centre of the table. The fresh air that hit Vivienne on entering the villa was wonderful and this came from a huge open-plan room with by-folding doors wrapping right around one side of the building from the salon, onto a grand terrace. Celeste and Vivienne sat facing the lake and Pierre sat down facing the villa. Vivienne expected he had had his fill of the view. The villa's décor was brazen, confident and gave a clear, no-messing message that supreme wealth lived here.

"My wife undertook all the interior design." Pierre had read Vivienne's thoughts. She did not respond. Vivienne did not particularly like the style and preferred ancient Egyptian architecture left where it belonged. Instead she smiled and nodded in approval.

The drinks were served by a little Spanish man whose wife appeared as well, they seemed to be the live-in couple who kept the place in order all year round. Delphine finally arrived, a little late in Vivienne's opinion and in Celeste's also, although she did not say so. Celeste's body language was so easy to read and quite amusing. Celeste immediately took out her dark Chanel sunglasses and put them on as Delphine arrived at the table. It was a clear put-down from Celeste and Delphine smirked.

"Ah darling. There you are. Vivienne, this is my wife Delphine. Delphine, this is Vivienne." Delphine did not attempt to shake Vivienne's hand and conveniently remained on the other side of the huge sun table. Without saying a word, she nodded towards Vivienne and then Celeste. She was a stunning woman. Delphine was tall, slim, extremely elegant and with a confident, sexy manner about her. It was immediately clear to Vivienne that her husband doted on her. He got up to pull out her chair, placing a loving kiss on her cheek as she sat down. Her long, dark curly hair flowed down her back and she was wearing a black sun dress which was backless and Pierre spent most of the lunch stroking her bare skin. This obviously annoyed Celeste and Vivienne could see that Delphine was enjoying Celeste's discomfort.

Delphine and Pierre were not an obvious match. One was tall, magnificent and graceful and the other was short and quite plain. Vivienne wondered if his money had made him all the more appealing to this woman and from this point onwards, Vivienne made a decision that she did not like Delphine much. The woman appeared far too detached as if she had far better things to be getting along with.

"You must come back here anytime Vivienne and use the swimming pool. It can get very hot down there in the town. Just get one of the boys to call up at the house and we will have everything prepared for you. Don't be a stranger." Vivienne felt that Pierre's invitation was genuine, but it was clear that Delphine did not second it. She stifled a yawn.

"Thank you Pierre. That is very kind of you," Vivienne replied genuinely. She liked Pierre very much.

They left Villa la Colonie and on the way down the long steep winding driveway, a young man was walking with a pretty girl in shorts.

"Ah, that's my grandson Victor." She made no reference to the girl, not knowing who it was or obviously wanting to know.

The car came to a halt and Celeste opened her window. The young man leaned in through the window and gave his grandmother a kiss on the cheek. It was obvious by Celeste's behaviour and body language that she adored her grandson and that he was the golden boy of the family.

"Victor. I would like you to meet my companion Vivienne. Vivienne, my gorgeous grandson Victor. Isn't he handsome?" Vivienne did not normally blush, but she did then for the first time as she had to agree with Celeste that her grandson was stunning. His features were angular with a rugged edge, he had a cleft in his large chin and his dark penetrating eyes stole her day.

"Yes Celeste. How do you do?" Vivienne asked, leaning over Celeste to shake his outstretched hand. Victor was obviously very comfortable with his grandmother and she did not flick an eyelid as he leant right over her body to shake Vivienne's hand, with his smiling eyes.

Victor winked at his grandmother and then as an afterthought, winked at Vivienne as he pulled his body back out of the car. He stood purposefully in front of the girl.

"I want to see you soon my boy. Come down to the apartment or tell me where you would like to dine out and we shall arrange it, won't we Vivienne?" She turned to Vivienne and Vivienne agreed.

"Of course Grandmamma. Whenever you say. I am here for the next four weeks." He turned then and taking the girls' hand, carried on walking up the hill towards the villa.

*

That evening Celeste was called out on business and Vivienne was given the night off. She was relieved. It had been a long, hot day and she did not feel like attending on Celeste. Vivienne took a long cool bath and decided to take a walk on the promenade to see if she could see Valentin.

Vivienne spent an hour walking up and down the east side of the promenade but Valentin did not show and finally she went home and had a fitful night's sleep.

Vivienne did not dream of Valentin that night. Instead she dreamt of Victor.

Chapter Fourteen

The infinity pool

The next day was even more glorious than the previous one and the sun came up at 5.00am across the lake as Celeste and Vivienne speed-walked around it. To increase her rhythm, Vivienne put on headphones with some upbeat music to help maintain her pace. Vivienne was losing weight rapidly with the healthy eating and four miles of early morning walks each day and her clothes we hanging off her. She reminded herself to buy a new set of clothes as soon as they reached Paris. Vivienne knew Celeste had many appointments with some famous couturiers that filled two weeks of diary appointments, which would give Vivienne plenty of time to sort out her own wardrobe.

Vivienne dressed in a breezy, coral silk dress with a slit up the side and Celeste commented on her dress and how it clung to her figure. Occasionally, Vivienne would catch Celeste glancing at her when she thought Vivienne was not looking and today was another occasion. This time, Vivienne caught Celeste's glance and Celeste looked away embarrassed.

Vivienne chose Celeste's clothes for the day and opened her fabulous wardrobe, running her hands across the plastic-topped black velvet hangers with her summer clothes carefully spaced and ordered in colour-coded fashion. Below, glass-topped drawers with matching silk scarves from Hermes and in the next wardrobe, was a fantastic display of handbags and another with shelves of shoes, white at the top and working down through the colours to black on the bottom shelf. When Celeste went shopping, she bought three of everything for each of her main homes. Pastor would take the clothes she wanted to transport between houses and soon Vivienne also got the hang of doing this. Like Lourel for Celeste, Matos would unpack Vivienne's clothes, carefully steam them before hanging them. Sometimes it felt that the staff were in control and Vivienne thought that in a way, they were. They ensured the house woke up and went to sleep. They ran the mechanics of the household. They were on a permanent stand-by, constantly ready to either provide breakfast, lunch or dinner or a light snack for pre-dinner drinks or for when a guest arrived. The houses were run like clockwork to Celeste's personal time table.

*

Vivienne chose a silver, lightweight silk suit for Celeste's meeting with her bankers in Zurich. She would go by car with Pastor and did not require Vivienne's assistance. It was suggested that Vivienne go to the villa to cool down if the sun got too hot as Pierre had suggested. Celeste told Vivienne to call the villa and the man servant would come down and collect her by car.

When Vivienne arrived at the villa, there was no one about except for the house staff. Master and Madame were apparently at work and if Vivienne needed anything she was just to call the red button on any phone positioned around the house. Vivienne had sent Matos out earlier in the morning for a couple of magazines and Vivienne headed for the pool changing room. She changed into a brand new white low cut Gottex bathing suit and lay down on a yellow and white striped sun lounger. The villa was also stunning on this side, with a commanding view of the lake. There was a garden room with by-folding doors opening onto a terrace so the pool could be used in summer or winter. To one side, a bar area with seating and loungers and a barbeque and situated in a prominent position was the most beautiful infinity swimming pool that Vivienne had ever seen. Its trick of the eye was at its best when floating on its glass surface where the water would expand into infinity into the trees, beyond the lake and up into the clouds of the magnificent Mont Blanc. Above the pool was a glass operated roof, which, to the touch of a button could slide away and expose the heat of the day. Thankfully, this action had already been performed for Vivienne and the swimming pool was peaceful and still except for the humming of the filter which lapped the water over the infinity edge every so often.

*

Vivienne looked about her and no-one was in sight – the house staff were well away on the other side of the house in their own private quarters. Vivienne was quite alone. She was boiling in her bathing suit. She looked longingly at the cool water of the pool. She wanted to feel the water against her skin and on an impulse, she removed her suit and dived into the pool, swimming the whole length under water. The cool water rippled over her body and cooled every crevice. On the floor of the pool, Vivienne swam above a tiled mermaid and smiled, thinking of how much it seemed that Celeste adored mermaids, they were everywhere.

As she came up for air, Vivienne saw a dark rippling shadow by the edge of the pool.

"Well hello again." It was Victor. He was standing in a white Lacoste polo shirt and navy blue linen shorts and bare feet. In his left hand, he was holding Vivienne's white bathing suit.

"Hi. Ah, you have my bathing suit. Could you pass it to me please?" Vivienne leant up to Victor to pass it down to her but he cruelly flicked it away.

"Well now. Maybe you will just have to come and get it from me." He turned and went to the back of the pool house in a dark shaded area that Vivienne had not noticed before. Upon a table, a book was opened flat, face down alongside an empty glass tumbler. Vivienne could not believe it. He had been here all the time and sneakily, had kept his presence secret, watching her, and even worse, while she had undressed and entered the pool.

"So. You got your eyes filled. Now the game is over, can I have my bathing suit?" Vivienne was a little frustrated and hated being teased.

"Why don't I just strip off too and join you?" he was really teasing Vivienne now and although he was absolutely stunning, Vivienne reminded herself of who he was. He also had a girlfriend.

"What about your girlfriend...?" Vivienne asked in an equally teasing manner. Not really caring about the answer.

"What girlfriend? Ah, yes, yesterday. She is just a friend. We are studying the same course and we help each other with our studies," he excused, shrugging his shoulders in a blazé action. *As if...* Vivienne thought.

He was a typical French, rich, smooth playboy and was only about nineteen, twenty at the most, and yet already a fully-fledged player of women. Vivienne would give him a gold medal for his ability to woo a female.

"You have a beautiful body Vivienne. It is wasted on my grandmother." Vivienne was shocked by this remark. Did he know then that his grandmother was a lesbian? Vivienne laughed this off.

"You should not say such things about your grandmother." Vivienne remarked and she was serious. Vivienne felt even more pity for Celeste now. She must be a joke in the family.

"Just please pass me back my bathing suit and you can go back to what you were doing and I can go back to what I was doing – okay?" Vivienne was beginning to cool down too much.

"Sure. Whatever." He threw down her bathing suit and picking up his book, left the pool room.

Vivienne was left feeling that she might have missed out on the best thing that had ever happened to her. *Damn – he was a good tease – too good.*

Chapter Fifteen

Victor Laisalle

Three weeks passed in daily clockwork routine with Celeste. Vivienne admired the older woman's dedication to her business. Often she would enter Celeste's rooms and she would be discussing a difficult tender or contract on the telephone that was being worked upon and her business acumen impressed Vivienne. Celeste was a problem-solver in business, never happy to be beaten on an obstacle, her will to find a solution was limitless.

This only increased Vivienne's admiration for her, and soon the incident in her bedroom was behind them. Celeste had not brought it up again. She had seen Vivienne's surprise and discomfort and must have decided that it was not worth upsetting her over it. Vivienne was grateful for this as it would have presented her with the difficult decision to leave Celeste which she did not want to do.

Even though it was Celeste's summer break, the woman worked. Most days she discussed business over lunch. Often Vivienne would accompany Celeste and she would be lying if she did not admit that she found the lunches extremely tedious. Most of Celeste's business was undertaken from London where she would speak English in most meetings, but when in Geneva, all business was undertaken in French and often Vivienne would lose the translation thread and wander off into thoughts of her own. She would find herself thinking of Timothy and where it had gone wrong. Then her mind would wander to Valentin and if she would ever bump into him again. Finally, her mind would rest on Victor. He was a stunning young man and without doubt, one of the most physically attractive of men Vivienne had ever met.

The memory of the day by the pool was imprinted on her mind and Vivienne realised that he had made more of an impact on her than she could admit. These three weeks only proved to Vivienne that he had been on her mind constantly. She also reminded herself that he had a girlfriend and taking a woman's man was not her style.

Another lunch business meeting was being arranged for the next day and Vivienne organised it exactly as Celeste wished.

"You know Vivienne. You have a day off sweetheart. You look tired and this business talk is not interesting for you. Why don't you go to the villa and swim? I will call Pierre and tell him you are going, yes?"

Dear Celeste. She wasn't all that bad and often thought of others in between her hectic work schedule.

Vivienne was happy to escape to La Colonie. If Vivienne had a choice of all of Celeste's homes, it would be this one. Its views were medicine and could heal any ailment.

A light lunch was made for Vivienne and she sat on the veranda eating silently. The sun beat down and it was too hot to sunbathe so she decided to swim in the pool. This time Vivienne kept her sunbathing suit on, and ensured she looked around the pool room in detail before taking her swim. No one was about. Vivienne decided to exercise thoroughly; her body was becoming very toned and firmer than ever and she swam forty lengths with ease.

"...no Victor. I won't. I won't leave Geneva, you promised me." An American girl's voice echoed from the salon room.

"I'm sorry Georgiana, but it's over. It's over."

"So who is it then? Suki? Oh, no, don't tell me, it's Camilla? It's Camilla isn't it?" Her high-pitched jealous tone was painful to hear. She was being dumped and was hurting. Vivienne knew this feeling only too well.

"No Georgiana. It's none of them. It's not about another woman. I just need time alone." Victor replied unconvincingly, Vivienne thought.

"Time alone? You? You are sex mad Victor. You've always been sex mad." Spat the girl.

"Well then. You will be happier without me then won't you?" his voice was flat and disinterested. He was leading her to the front door.

"Hi José. Could you please order a taxi for the girl? Thank you." Vivienne heard the click of the house phone. She did not know whether to get out and hide or to stay in the pool. She did not move.

"Fine. Have it your way. You will be sorry. Just you wait and see." Vivienne heard the slam of the front door. Silence.

Uncomfortably, Vivienne decided to swim, her head down in the water, moving silently up and down the pool. She knew that Victor was still in the villa and felt guilty that she had overheard his private discussion.

Suddenly Vivienne heard a splash behind her and a dark shape moving slowing and swiftly under the water. It's smooth, long, proficient underwater strides coming closer and closer. It was Victor. A naked Victor.

Vivienne bit her lip as the pool water dripped from her tanned face. She did not know how she was going to keep her cool over this gorgeous man who no longer had a girlfriend or for that matter – clothes.

He came up to the surface, gracefully, not spluttering water like Vivienne had. He was not out of breath at all after swimming the whole length of the pool underwater. His tanned muscles glistened as the water trickled from his swelling shoulders. He flicked his head in one large movement to remove the excess water. Droplets fell from his long dark lashes and perfectly formed nose.

Victor was silent. His eyes stared at Vivienne. He was intoxicating. His arms outstretched around her to capture her, his hands touching the sides of the pool. Vivienne could not move. She could not breathe.

Her gaze locked into his, everything around them disappeared. If Celeste had walked into the pool room at that moment, Vivienne would not have cared.

Victor's eyes were searching. He found the weakness there deep within her. He knew he had her. He carried Vivienne with ease from the pool. Vivienne in her white swimsuit and him naked, over to the reserve sun loungers at the back of the pool room.

The darkness there was secretive and he laid her down and silently removed her swimsuit. His nakedness reminded Vivienne of Michael Angelo's 'David'. His form was perfect. He made love to Vivienne then with a level of expertise that she did not believe could be possible in one so young. He was an expert lover, and moved around her body with skill and confidence. His tongue was thick and hot and he licked and sucked with relish. He took Vivienne's nipples into his mouth and bit them until her back arched, ready for him to enter her. He did so with ease – slowly making love to her whilst looking deep into her eyes and kissing Vivienne on her mouth, darting his hot tongue between her lips and entangling his tongue with hers.

Vivienne was blown away by the passion of the man. She did not care that she was probably his second conquest that week if not that day.

Chapter Sixteen

Rue de Courcelle's, Paris – late August

After two months in Geneva, Celeste declared that they were to leave for Paris the next day. Vivienne left behind Valentin whom she only saw that once, but more importantly, Victor.

Victor and Vivienne had had many more secret assignations after that second time in the pool room and he would take any opportunity to come and see his grandmother whenever he could, of course to meet Vivienne and secretly kiss when Celeste's back was turned.

Even Celeste remarked that she had never seen so much of him, but thankfully she never guessed that there was anything going on between the two of them. They had made a pact on that second passionate day by the pool that they would not mention it to anyone, especially Celeste.

The private jet took off from Geneva airport early on a late August morning. As they flew over Geneva bay, Vivienne thought about the wonderful summer that she would never forget.

They landed at Charles De Gaulle airport and once again, Pastor was there to greet them on the forecourt. As before, their passports were checked by airport officials before they were allowed to disembark from the plane.

Celeste's palatial penthouse apartment on Rue de Courcelle's was parallel to the Avenue de Champs-Élysées and forked off the roundabout of the Arc de Triomphe. It is one of the most prestigious locations in Paris and the views from Vivienne's private rooms on the fourteenth floor, gave a bird's eye view of the lit up Arc de Triomphe.

Celeste's private rooms were decorated with blue and gold peacocks, on the walls, bed, headboards and curtains. The silk opulence was everywhere and very typically Parisian. No expense had been spared in this apartment and the inside did perfect justice to the colonial exterior. Marble walls and floors left a cool feel under foot and the plunge pool on the veranda was a welcome relief from the hot sun.

It was wonderful to experience each of Celeste's homes, one after the other, yet the level of wealth never ceased to amaze Vivienne. There seemed to be no limit to what she could afford. Every home was efficiently serviced, maintained, staffed and prepared for her arrival.

The main salon with its impressive by-folding doors overlooked a veranda of palms, terracotta urns and an amazing mermaid fountain, with a trickle of water streaming into a pool of water lilies. Further down the veranda, a pergola covered with begonias sat over a beautifully welcoming plunge pool for quick refreshment.

Huge double sun loungers in white with black trim were positioned carefully around its perimeter. The views from the external balcony were incredible. Vivienne could see the Eiffel Tower and the lush gardens in front of it, then a maze of roads and narrow streets and roof tops and roof top gardens spread about the city.

Paris was the best place to eat in the world and the restaurants were many and superb. When Celeste shopped, Vivienne shopped and together they visited Chanel, Hermes and Versace in Montmartre and had lunch at the Ritz. When she had time, Vivienne would stop in Benetton or Zara and pick up a few smaller items of clothing for herself.

Vivienne never took her situation for granted and recognised how fortunate she was. She felt that God was looking down on her after such a terrible nine years with her ex-husband. She hoped that this was her chance to live a little.

Vivienne wondered if it had changed her at all, all this extravagance. Was she the same person as the first day she arrived for her interview, stopping at Richoux for a coffee she could barely afford? Having no money had made her feel small, incapable, afraid and unconfident. Ugly too. She had not been able to dress like the woman with the pearls and the alligator shoes. Not that she would welcome a pair of alligator shoes, but still, Vivienne was very different now, and not just physically.

She no longer wore her Citizen watch, wearing now a Cartier encrusted with diamonds, another gift from Celeste. She was perfectly groomed and maintained. She was slim, toned and capable. A new Vivienne had been born.

Celeste was not a snob. This was not possible as she had been born into wealth and knew no other way of living. Of course, she saw others live different lives and she knew she was exceedingly fortunate, but this was put down to her hard work and good choices in business which Vivienne found quite frustrating. Vivienne herself enjoyed what she was receiving but she knew it was all on loan.

At some point just like Cinderella, the whole experience would end and everything would have to be returned. Maintaining this sense of realism amongst everyday exclusive living was Vivienne's mainstay, and helped her to focus on what she was building for the future.

Vivienne became proficient in knowing how to behave in different environments, whereas Celeste was just naturally dismissive. To her, everyone was of service to her in some form or another. She was at the top of the pecking order, she knew no other way. Celeste had a knack of flicking her hand up as a means of dismissal. It was all she knew.

Eventually, Celeste realised that Vivienne was sensitive to this kind of behaviour and recognised that at these times Vivienne had a way of dismissing Celeste in her own way.

In time, Vivienne had changed Celeste also. Celeste became more careful about how she addressed people and especially her staff.

On one occasion, Vivienne threatened to leave if she did not apologise to Lourel. Celeste had sent him away because he had forgotten to hand pick the raisins from her breakfast cereal. Celeste hated raisins. Once, Vivienne had walked into the kitchen in Mayfair to make herself a cup of tea and Lourel was sitting hunched over the marble worktop with a whole bag of muesli spread out, picking out the raisins one by one.

*

They had been in Paris two weeks when Celeste hurt her back following their daily morning walk on the Champs-Élysées. This was their new habitual walking ground accompanied by the ever faithful Matos.

"Vivienne. Bring me my diary will you dear? I need the number of my masseuse. My back feels like it is about to break."

Vivienne dutifully brought her diary, thinking that her masseuse was based in Paris. To her surprise, she was based in Harley Street in London and would have to be flown out by Celeste's own jet to fix her back.

This was the kind of wild extravagance that occurred on a daily basis.

Chapter Seventeen

Marlene Forsythe

The day Marlene Forsythe arrived was the day Vivienne's life changed forever. The erotic, older woman brought out a duality inside Vivienne that she never knew existed. Marlene was without doubt the most stunning woman Vivienne had ever seen.

She arrived at the penthouse wearing a thin, almost transparent white silk jumpsuit and dangerously high white wedge sandals.

Golden, defined muscles bulged from her slim frame. Large, bra-less implanted breasts stretched the silk cloth of her suit and her nipples stuck out like gobstoppers.

Her shiny, long brunette hair hung in one long curl over one shoulder and bounced as she walked, on her massive bosom. Her taut neck, was long and sleek. Her striking, high cheekbones were carefully dusted with rouge to match her full lips and her cat-like eyes shone in mischief. Her high, arched, thick eyebrows were heavily defined.

The Comtesse lit up when Marlene walked into the room. So did Vivienne. According to Celeste, she ran a hugely successful and exclusive gym in Harley Street serving the rich and famous. Her membership fees were extortionate to purposely maintain exclusivity.

As she placed down her white leather holdall, her hands appeared strong, yet delicate. Her long fingers had a perfectly applied French manicure. She adeptly unzipped her bag and retrieved some exotic looking oils and presses. Her presence was assertive and she exuded an air of control and professionalism.

"Darling Celeste......how are you dear?" she asked Celeste in a patronising, yet considerate tone.

"Oh Marlene sweetie. I have hurt my back again. Can you fix it my love?" Celeste whimpered. Celeste was in bed and Marlene leaned down to kiss her cheek. Celeste got a good eye fill of Marlene's cleavage.

"Now. Strip off and let's take a look." Marlene clapped her hands together. She swiftly tied up her hair and secured it with a grip. Vivienne watched Marlene's every move intently. Quietly. Mesmerised. Her neck was now fully visible. It's long, narrow delicateness had flawless skin. Vivienne swallowed loudly and hoped no one had heard her. She was staring. She couldn't help it.

"Celeste dear. Are you going to introduce me to your little protégé here, or am I going to have to kiss her on the mouth to stop her gaping at me."

Vivienne snapped her mouth shut and turned away, blushing. Celeste peered over Marlene's shoulder to see Vivienne's face, but thankfully, she had missed her blushing moment.

"This is Vivienne, Marlene, my new companion. Isn't she gorgeous? Aren't I lucky darling?" Celeste gushed.

"I think I'm rather jealous actually. You know how much I just adore blondes. You brought her here just to tease me, didn't you darling, you naughty thing." She declared and winked at me.

Vivienne felt completely out of her league with this woman. Marlene spoke to Celeste like a close friend, yet she was just another member of staff to Celeste. Her audacity and confidence was alluring and she practically had Celeste eating out of her hand.

Vivienne was madly attracted to her as she expected Celeste was also. She did not know how Celeste could stand having Marlene's hands massage her body in such an erotic manner.

Celeste moaned and groaned, and Vivienne became a little uncomfortable in the room. She felt like an intruder. She finally left them to it and went to her room; Vivienne could not stand it anymore.

147

Now Vivienne knew why Celeste had flown Marlene in. She was worth every penny.

Celeste and Marlene were together for several hours in Celeste's room and later that night, Celeste took them all out to dinner at Le Crillion. Marlene and Celeste chatted happily all evening. Marlene gave nutritional advice and took over the ordering of the food. Celeste and Vivienne were both entranced and just watched Marlene dominate the evening.

Marlene glanced frequently at Vivienne in an odd manner at times. Vivienne felt unsure of how to respond. This was an area of complete inexperience and complexity for Vivienne. She was also worried that maybe Celeste might see that Marlene found her mildly interesting.

Vivienne tried not to encourage Marlene's attention. She would be the one left living with Celeste afterwards, not Marlene. Life alone with Celeste could at times be testing.

Vivienne found Marlene fascinating. She was an exotic bird that Vivienne wanted to touch and stroke. Vivienne did not mind one bit that it was apparent that Marlene seemed to have taken an obvious liking to her. Celeste and Vivienne enjoyed their new female companion greatly. Celeste had booked Marlene into the George VI hotel which was not far from their home and the three dined out constantly. Marlene was a marvellous and fresh addition to the twosome and where Vivienne had suffered weeks and weeks in the older woman's company. Except for Valentin and Victor, Vivienne thought she would have gone mad with boredom.

The new threesome would shop for fitness clothing, nutritional foods and supplements, all of which ended up in the bin by the end of their trip to Paris. Marlene was an expert at spending other people's money. She hit the menu wherever they dined, ordering fresh lobster and truffles or caviar mousselines with langoustines. She sat for hours explaining the importance of certain minerals or proteins to an extremely attentive Celeste.

One night, Marlene returned back to Rue de Courcelles for a nightcap. Celeste told Vivienne to retire.

Vivienne did not hear Marlene leave that night and she could only assume that she had slept with Celeste as there was no other guest room.

Vivienne did not sleep well. She was jealous.

*

The next morning, Celeste did not appear from her room, nor did Lourel disturb her. Marlene was in with Celeste. There was no morning walk.

Their daily routine had been abandoned for the first time in nearly three months. Vivienne was so used to her new routine and not knowing what to do with herself at 5.30am on a Sunday morning, decided to walk out alone.

On return to the apartment, Vivienne heard Marlene's lively feet in the kitchen making coffee. She knew it was Marlene. She had a manner that could not be mistaken. Her movements were light, fast and energetic. She was half- naked when Vivienne entered the kitchen.

The house staff were nowhere to be seen. Not that it would have mattered to Marlene. Marlene was a woman who was extremely confident of her body and proud to show it to anyone who desired to take a look.

Vivienne watched her sexy features; she had nothing on except for soft, see-through panties, the outline of her sex clear to see. Vivienne was mesmerized, watching her take some juice out of the fridge, drinking straight from the bottle. She poured a cup of coffee. Her breasts bounced in a way that excited Vivienne so that she could not take her eyes off her. Vivienne had never been so silent.

"Good morning sweetie. Fancy some coffee?" she took a sip from her steaming cup.

"No I'm fine thanks," Vivienne replied, removing the headset from her neck and the iPod from her arm.

"You're a good girl aren't you? Already had your morning exercise, I see. You should come to my gym sweetie and I will whip that figure of yours into shape in no time."

"What would you change about my body?" Vivienne replied building confidence, and genuinely curious about what she thought about her.

"Well, you are stunning already my sweet, but I could spend time on you, firm you up a little more and maybe some massage?" She offered. She was rich. She had to be with an address such as hers. Yet, oddly, she was offering Vivienne her services.

"You want me to join your gym?" Vivienne asked.

"Well, we can see about that, at least come down and take a look; I have a lovely penthouse on the top floor. Take a look around when you're back in London." She eyed Vivienne with those dangerous, tiger-like eyes and taking a fresh orange that she had just peeled, took a segment and put it onto her tongue suggestively. Vivienne could not deny that she was intrigued and terrified all at the same time. Vivienne found her difficult to decipher. This complex and highly sexual woman could have implied a thousand things.

She winked, turned and left. Vivienne watched her bottom as she walked across the salon back to Celeste's bedroom. The muscles of her backside were rippling, the long muscles of her beautiful calves tensed as she walked. She glided like a panther. Her hair rippled down her back. She was an incredible sight and Vivienne would never forget that first semi-naked image of Marlene. It became imprinted on her mind forever.

Chapter Eighteen

Marlene at Grosvenor Square

Summer was soon over. Celeste and Vivienne flew back to London and soon were settled back into their usual routine at Grosvenor Square. Memories of Geneva haunted Vivienne daily. Sweet memories of Victor and hedonistic, lustful thoughts of Marlene.

Esther was ecstatic to see Vivienne and she took her for long walks in Hyde Park during Celeste's siestas. Vivienne had missed Esther terribly and promised to get her a dog passport the next time they had to go abroad.

In early September, Vivienne was allowed a week off to see her family, visit friends and sort out her financial affairs. Vivienne left Mayfair in her new S class Mercedes convertible. The hood was down and the fresh breeze blew through her hair. She put her foot to the gas and left London and headed for Hampshire. It was not hard to leave Celeste, but it was awful to leave Esther. The little dog had wined while Vivienne had packed her case and cried and scratched at the garden door as Vivienne left.

It was not long, just a few days, before Celeste was on the phone.

"Vivienne darling, darling. I miss you so. Please come home to me sweetheart. Esther misses you too." Poor Esther, Vivienne had been away for nearly three months and as soon as she arrived back in London she had to leave again. Her heart lurched for the little creature.

"Of course Celeste, I will be back tomorrow morning, I just have to finish my affairs here." Vivienne hung up. Her house was finally sold and she would soon have to move her things out. She no longer wanted anything from the house. It was filled with furniture from catalogues and now she could afford far better and more beautiful possessions. She decided to leave everything to her ex-husband and take just her personal possessions to Celeste's house in Mayfair until she found another more suitable home.

Chapter Nineteen

Spring

Vivienne returned to Grosvenor Square and to Celeste and continued their routine until one evening, Vivienne received a call from Marlene. She had invited her to come and see her at her gym.

It was early afternoon on a balmy September day as Vivienne stepped out of a black cab outside Marlene's Gym on Harley Street. The building was a tall, narrow, cream terrace house made of stone with two marble columns gracing an entrance porch and wide stone steps leading to the pavement. It reminded Vivienne of an old upstairs downstairs building, with a basement below ground. In the porch, a large glass lantern pooled light illuminating a beautifully shiny, black, painted door. The door was off the latch and she pushed it open. The hallway was magnificent with a black and white large entrance hall. A pretty young receptionist sat at a high desk which had an enormous display of orchids in a clear glass bowl.

In one room, several people were using some gym equipment and Vivienne contained her stare as she saw Chris Martin. In another room, a Yoga class was in session with just three customers who were stretching on white leather thin mattresses.

The pretty receptionist pressed the lift button and asked Vivienne to enter. Vivienne was a little bemused, but did as she was told. In the lift, the girl turned a key on a button with a plaque next to it which said "Private – Penthouse Only" and closed the gated doors on her.

Vivienne arrived at the penthouse. It occupied the whole length and width of the building. Everywhere was white marble, white furniture, huge white blinds and white drapes at the windows. The drapes hung from a vaulted ceiling to the floor and were maybe thirty feet in length.

The dining room had a white, shiny dining table with cowhide high-backed dining chairs and to one wall, a Bang & Olufsen CD player playing soft music. To the right, a stunning black and white marble kitchen in a minimalistic style with a floor to ceiling champagne chiller which took pride of place. To the left, was a lounge with many white sofas spread around a magnificent fireplace with a low, white shiny table in the centre.

Then there was Marlene. She glided across the room to greet Vivienne, her hips swinging in their usual seductive manner.

"Darling. Come in darling. My darling Vivienne." Vivienne was surprised she wasn't wearing a gym outfit. She felt stupid standing there in a tight black leotard and trainers. Marlene was wearing long, white cheesecloth pants and a white clingy vest, her breasts were barely covered and her nipples stood to attention. Her glossy, long hair curled together at their ends and hung over one shoulder in her usual glamorous manner. Her makeup was simple but sublime and her long nails were painted in a soft beige, along with her long toe nails. Around her wrists, fingers and neck were silver Cartier pieces that made her look simple and elegant. She matched her room perfectly.

"Marlene. It is so wonderful to be here at last. I have missed you." Vivienne stated honestly and hugged her. Her breasts pushed into Vivienne's as they air kissed each other. She took the opportunity to whisper into Vivienne's ear. "Come – let's go get some champagne", and taking Vivienne by the hand, dragged her down the corridor to the kitchen.

"Oh darling. You do look gorgeous in your gym gear – I should have told you, it's my day off today. When are you going to come and join the gym? I would love to get to work on your body sweetheart." She blew Vivienne a kiss as she opened the glass cupboard and retrieved two crystal flutes. She poured the champagne and they clinked glasses.

"To freedom in love" she said and sipped her champagne. Vivienne had left Celeste watching the lunchtime news. She had told her she was joining a gym in Belgravia. Thankfully, Celeste had appeared disinterested and had made no connection to Marlene's gym in Harley Street.

Vivienne looked into Marlene's eyes as she took another sip of champagne. The bubbles danced upon her tongue. She licked her lips as some champagne had lingered there. Marlene watched intently. She leaned in and kissed Vivienne on the lips, softly.

"You missed a drop" she said, licking Vivienne's lips and kissing her again. Her husband was down in the gym and Vivienne felt uncomfortable knowing they were alone together, but Marlene was oblivious to this.

Vivienne could smell Marlene's beautiful scent, she was wearing Balenciaga by Balenciaga and the heady scent filled her nostrils and Vivienne had an incredible urge to run her fingers through Marlene's hair and untangle it from its long thick curl. Vivienne loved Marlene's wild features. She was a natural beauty, but with cosmetics, designer clothes and professional hair sessions, Marlene was a vision of perfection. Vivienne had a secret urge to see Marlene free again – naked again – but this time, just for herself.

"What are you thinking Vivienne? You are deep in thought." Marlene looked up into Vivienne's face.

"Do you really want to know Marlene?" Vivienne challenged. Vivienne was becoming a new woman now. She was experimenting, learning about men as much as women. She was embracing her sexuality and the effect it had. Vivienne was realising rapidly that her body and her mind had a secret power.

"You have changed Vivienne. You are different. What has happened to our sweet, innocent Vivienne?" Marlene teased.

Vivienne glanced at Marlene's breasts and looked up her. Marlene had read her thoughts.

"Take them Vivienne. They are yours." She was challenging Vivienne again and Vivienne wanted to. *So much.*

Vivienne took one of her breasts and squeezed firmly and kissed Marlene hard on the mouth, biting her lip a little until it bled. Marlene pulled away, sucking the blood from her lip.

"My, my. Vivienne. I shall have to watch you." She was excited. Vivienne had no idea how to make love to a woman. She felt a little awkward. But with Marlene it did not matter. She seemed experienced in seducing women. Vivienne was in safe hands. Marlene was older by seven years and those seven years were being demonstrated to Vivienne now.

Marlene put down Vivienne's champagne glass and taking her hand, took her to her bedroom. Everything was in white with a huge bed with soft draped curtains surrounding a metal canopy.

Marlene undressed and the vision of her curves came back to Vivienne from when she had first seen her nakedness in Celeste's kitchen in Paris. The woman's curves were deep and hard with narrow hips and long muscled legs. She had a tiny waist with a defined twelve pack on her stomach and a seductive 'v' where her rib cage held those enormous breasts.

Vivienne could not say whether Marlene seduced her or if Vivienne seduced Marlene. They were wrapped in each other's arms and made love all afternoon. Licking, sucking and pulling at each other.

Vivienne fell in love with Marlene that day and felt she would kill any man or woman for that matter who attempted to make love to Marlene again.

Chapter Twenty

Interception – summer

September was a wonderful month in London that year. Marlene and Vivienne had a love affair. Her husband Gene was oblivious to their suddenly formed friendship. Vivienne took Marlene away from her home and business at odd hours of the day and night. She managed to slip away from Celeste when she slept, either after lunch or during the hours in the middle of the night. Only the staff at Grosvenor Square watched Vivienne come and go and she took them cakes and small gifts to buy their confidence.

One morning at Grosvenor Square, Vivienne received a letter delivered on a silver platter by Matos. She picked it up from him and he looked embarrassed. The letter had been opened already, Vivienne immediately recognised Marlene's handwriting.

"Who has read this?" Vivienne demanded to the reddening Matos.

"Her Excellency, Miss Vivienne." He left hastily from the room before Vivienne could ask further questions.

Vivienne opened the letter slowly, dreading the words inside. Not because she did not feel love for Marlene, but because she dreaded the words she had used to write to her, knowing Celeste had already read it.

My darling Vivienne,

I have not been able to sleep at nights thinking of our days together.

Gene makes regular passes at me and I am unable to allow him to touch me after the passion you and I have shared together.

My sweet, adorable, beautiful Vivienne. I have to confess that I have fallen in love with you. Tell me that you feel the same way, darling Vivienne. I beg that you feel the same way. I have made love to women and men, but never have I tasted one as sweet as you. You are my love, my life, my Vivienne. Vivienne. Vivienne. Tell me you will come to me soon. I am waiting.

Impatiently yours, Marlene. Xxxxxx

Vivienne folded the letter and taking some matches, set light to it and watched as it burnt to cinders in her bathroom sink. What on earth was she going to say to Celeste. The old woman was sure to dismiss her now.

Vivienne dressed carefully, solemnly, slowing down the inevitable.

Celeste was sitting at her desk in her study when Vivienne went upstairs. She knew this was a display of anger and control. Vivienne knew this meant business and she dreaded what was to come next.

"Ah. Vivienne. I want to talk to you. Sit down please." Celeste had not looked up and it felt like the first day when Vivienne had been interviewed four months previously. She sat down obediently, waiting to be spoken to.

"I was given a letter by accident it appears. A letter from Marlene addressed to you. I read it of course. I am not happy Vivienne. You have disappointed me greatly. I don't care about Marlene. Marlene is of no concern to me. Nothing surprises me about that woman. But you Vivienne. I did not expect it from you. I can only assume that that woman has seduced you. Has she seduced you Vivienne?" Celeste folded her arms as she looked up at Vivienne. Vivienne did not miss this gesture of closed body language.

"I am sorry Celeste. I truly did not mean to hurt you. I think......I think that I am in love with Marlene." Vivienne whispered.

"I see. Well. I cannot allow that. It is not possible to love that woman. She is a seductress and you will only be one of thousands that she has seduced in that tower of hers. I command that you never see her again Vivienne or I shall be forced to let you go. Do you understand?"

"I..." Vivienne began.

"Pack your things Vivienne. We shall be departing for Geneva tomorrow morning. I have just this minute sent on Lourel and Pastor in the car."

All Vivienne could think about was Marlene and Esther. Marlene because Vivienne knew she would be angry with Celeste and Esther because she had not had time to arrange her pet Passport.

"Of course Celeste. Whatever you say." Vivienne stood and left her office.

Chapter Twenty-One

Victor's Declaration

September was quiet in Geneva. Most of the tourists had gone home and just residents were left. Celeste was exceptionally quiet and the mornings were painfully long, lunches spent in fabulous settings with fine food and wine wasted on the two of them, and the evenings dragged on. They hardly spoke to one another and Vivienne felt bereft. Marlene was far behind her in London and their passion had only just begun. Vivienne wanted to be in her arms – she longed to be in her embrace, smelling her sweet, floral scent. Instead, Vivienne retired early to bed in order to dream of her.

*

Celeste was very upset and withdrawn and often dismissed Vivienne from her company. Vivienne knew that she had gotten away with it this time, but there would not be a next time, she was sure of it. Celeste seemed heartbroken and often Vivienne would catch Celeste watching her with a tear in her eye. Vivienne did not feel bad towards Celeste. The older woman had tried to seduce Vivienne herself. She just felt pity for her. Vivienne pitied that Celeste had to buy her company and that no one truly loved the woman. Not even her family. They never came to visit unless she demanded their attention. It was painful to see her treated so, but she was a hard woman. A woman who had never truly been in love with anyone or truly loved in return.

*

The months passed. December came and went solemnly with just a phone call to her parents and friends to wish them a Merry Christmas.

January, February, March, April all passed with no visits, no entertainment and Vivienne missed Esther more and more. She asked Celeste if she could arrange a pet Passport for Esther and the woman had refused, telling Vivienne that Esther got travel sick. Vivienne did not believe her. Vivienne truly felt that Celeste was even jealous of the time spent with Esther and wanted Vivienne all to herself. Vivienne began to hate Celeste's insane jealousy and the constant hold she had over her.

Marlene was becoming a fading memory. No doubt she had moved on by now with someone else or was back in her husband's arms. Vivienne knew she had to forget her, but found it difficult. All her mail was read before she had seen it, all of it opened blatantly now and left on the sideboard in the salon rather than presented on a platter as it had been before. Vivienne thought that even Matos no longer wanted the humiliation of presenting her with her opened mail. It was clear the house staff had been told to deliver all mail straight to Celeste.

Vivienne was sure that Celeste was not enjoying this long stint in Geneva. She constantly remarked how magical London was at Christmas and seemed to take it out on Vivienne that they were stuck in a summer resort in mid-winter. It was Vivienne's fault. She had betrayed Celeste and her contract. A part of Vivienne did not care. It had been worth it although she knew that there would never be another woman for her. It was Marlene or no woman. Vivienne was not a lesbian, she was sure of it. Marlene was exceptional and would attract women or men to her quite easily – she could have anyone she wanted. Vivienne was sure that this was partly the reason her fitness business was so successful. Her figure and her looks were the mastermind behind its success.

Celeste had parted Marlene and Vivienne and her plan was working.

As the long months passed, Vivienne no longer lusted after Marlene or felt that she was in love with her anymore. All that remained was just a faint, sweet memory of time spent with Marlene.

Celeste was winning. Instead, loneliness and a sense of quietness fell over Vivienne and she even became a little withdrawn and Celeste began to notice. Vivienne was looking pale and thin and no longer cared for her health. She forgot to eat and only ate when she was out with Celeste and, very small amounts. Vivienne drank less too. Celeste was being cruel and had made a decision to bring Vivienne to Switzerland against her will and away from her family at Christmas when she needed them most. All of this compounded into self-neglect and Vivienne began to turn into a shadow of her former vibrant self.

Even for Celeste, there was no family here in Geneva. Pierre, Delphine and Victor were in New York as they always were during winter, running their own businesses and private affairs from there. Victor was at Browns University and studying for his final year.

Being cooped up in Geneva away from London nightlife was difficult for Celeste, Vivienne could see that. She talked often of Christmas in London and the lights and the Christmas trees and Vivienne could see that Celeste longed to be back there.

On Quai Wilson, Vivienne watched as the Christmas lights were hung up on street lamp posts and eventually taken down. Snow came to the mountains and finally left as spring came. Vivienne looked forward to their morning walks which were often carried out in silence. The lake would be quite still and lifeless and it represented exactly how Vivienne felt inside. The only life around her was the crocus flowers springing to life along the grass verges and in the park of the United Nations Building.

Vivienne missed Esther awfully. She would call the house in Mayfair and get Rosa to put the little dog to the telephone and Vivienne would talk to her. Esther would then bark and twirl around in circles apparently, twisting her little bum sideways as she would when she was deliriously happy. Vivienne and Esther would be content with this for a while, but it would not last.

Vivienne could not bear to see people with their dogs in the park or at restaurants perched on their laps. A pull in her heart would go out to Esther and she decided that she was her dog as Celeste never once mentioned her.

Summer returned to Quai Wilson and with it the tourists in their hundreds, occupying the lake with their yachts and walking the promenade in front of the house. Vivienne often looked out for Valentin, but still he did not appear. Even he would have been a diversion to her dull routine.

One particularly hot day in late June Vivienne decided to go up to the villa alone. Celeste did not want to go as Pierre and his wife had not yet arrived from

New York. Victor was apparently holidaying in St. Tropez with family of a friend and would not be here until July with his parents. Vivienne knew he would be there for the whole summer and partly looked forward to seeing him again.

Vivienne arrived at the villa and the fresh lake breeze that wafted up the mountainside welcomed her back. The house was clean and quiet. The staff greeted her warmly, glad to see someone again. They brought refreshments and retired to their private quarters.

Vivienne went to the pool room, all was silent. She glanced over to the relaxation area where she and Victor had made love and smiled inwardly. At least she still had some secrets from Celeste.

Vivienne stripped and dived into the pool naked. There was no one about, she was sure of it this time and she was more confident of her nakedness and the feel of the cool water against her clammy, hot skin was superbly refreshing.

Vivienne frolicked about in the water and pretended to be like the mermaid that was at the bottom of the pool. She nicknamed her Oceana and made up an imaginary story for her. Oceana was captured from the sea by a wicked witch and made to live inside the swimming pool. She became Vivienne's friend here in Geneva and Oceana loved to swim with Vivienne – her new best friend.

*

There was a splash and Vivienne's mind reeled. It couldn't be. It was. Victor had dived naked into the pool and was swimming closer and closer to Vivienne under the water. His hair had grown and was long and sleek in the water with each stride. His dark, sparkling, smiling eyes caught Vivienne's horror and then he held her, under the water and kissed her. Bubbles went up above their heads as together, they came to the surface. Vivienne thought she was dreaming. The day had been hot, maybe she was hallucinating.

It was not a dream or a hallucination. Victor was older. It had only been a year, but he was even more stunning than the summer before. His features were more defined and now he had a stubble. His new long wavy hair glistened as droplets of water ran from his thick black locks.

He carried Vivienne from the pool, they were silent. Vivienne was sure she was still dreaming. She had dreamt so many times of that time in the pool and it must have been the confusion of losing Marlene and the strain that followed that made her imagine this was now happening.

Victor made love to Vivienne like the first time, wet skin on wet skin, their bodies sliding over each other and they both climaxed together. They did not care if anyone caught them, they were lost in the moment, so happy to be loved and love in return. He reached for some towels afterwards and dried Vivienne gently.

"My sweet Vivienne. How I missed you. I came over to Geneva to surprise you. Are you happy?" he rubbed his own body with another towel. His newly attained bulging muscles rippled as his arms worked. He had filled out handsomely.

"Yes. Of course I am happy to see you. You have changed. You look different." Vivienne meant it.

"Good different I hope?" his eyes were laughing at her, like they always did.

"No girlfriend this summer?" Vivienne teased.

"No my sweet. No girl but you."

"Yet." Vivienne pushed.

"I never stopped thinking about you the whole winter. I have not been the same since last summer. I promise you. And you? Have you not had a lover between last summer and now?" he quizzed.

"No-one that you should worry yourself over Victor. No." Of course she had been with Marlene, but she wanted to keep Marlene to herself. For now. Anyhow, Marlene was probably making love with Gene, so why not spend time with Victor.

"We can spend the whole summer together Vivienne. There is nothing stopping us. My parents won't be here for another two weeks and I can wrap my grandmother around my little finger. Just you watch." Vivienne believed him. He could wrap her around his little finger if he wanted to.

"I want to tell you something Vivienne. Please, let us go and drink some iced tea." They dressed then and went to sit on the veranda in the sun.

Victor took Vivienne's hand and looked lovingly into her eyes. For a moment Vivienne had trouble taking him seriously, it was so unlike him.

"Vivienne. I think I have fallen in love with you. Promise me you will not break my heart. No girl has ever had a confession of love from me before. Can I entrust you with my heart Vivienne, or will you break it?" he was on his knees now, in front of Vivienne, the lake and mountains a backdrop to his declaration.

"Victor. You are so young. I am nearly ten years older than you. You are not in love with me. You think you are, maybe just a little." Vivienne ran her fingers through his thick hair and looked at his young features, still turning into a beautiful young man. He had fallen for an older woman. The oldest trick in the book.

Vivienne felt like she was robbing him of his youth, just as Celeste had tried to do to her. Yet, this was different.

"No, I do not care about your age Vivienne. You are the most beautiful, stunning woman I have ever seen and I want to ask my parents for your hand in marriage. Do you accept?" Vivienne was genuinely shocked.

"No Victor. I cannot accept. You are still at University, your parents will be livid and Celeste will cast you off without a penny. No, I am sorry, I cannot accept. Don't you see? Celeste is my employer and your grandmother. Some things are not so straight forward Victor." Vivienne was honoured that he had asked her, but it was out of the question.

"You are refusing me Vivienne?" he was hurt, it was as if Vivienne had slapped him across his face. He stood now and turned towards the lake. His head was partially downcast and he ran his fingers angrily through his hair. His family still owned him and owned the woman he loved.

Vivienne stood up and closed the distance between them.

"You will find someone of your own age Victor. Someone young, beautiful, clever and intelligent. She is out there waiting for you. You just need to find her. You are too young to marry. You need to live your life. I do not want to rob you of that. In time, you will see that I am right." Vivienne turned him around to face her. Tears had welled up in his eyes. Vivienne kissed his closed mouth for the last time and left.

Chapter Twenty-Two

Paris

It was not easy to leave Victor. Vivienne adored him and she had wanted to spend the whole summer making love with him. But not on the basis that he wanted to marry her. It would have been cruel.

Vivienne was flattered, of course, but she did not want Celeste as her mother-in-law. She knew too much about the woman and it just would not have been right. Vivienne had been looking forward to spending time at the villa that summer, but sadly this would be a place that she could no longer visit without Celeste.

Celeste decided to stay in Geneva for four more weeks and Vivienne also stayed dutifully at Celeste's side, walking with her, reading to her, massaging her and they talked about life and Celeste's childhood. Vivienne was fascinated about learning about Celeste's early childhood in the Parisian countryside. It had sounded idyllic.

Vivienne asked Celeste how she had met Gaston her husband and what her wedding was like and where she went on honeymoon. There had only ever been a brotherly love for Gaston, but Vivienne could tell she had loved him and he her. She talked about what life would have been like if they had been King and Queen of France and living in the Palace of Versailles. Celeste and Vivienne watched French films together and Vivienne's French improved dramatically that summer.

It was not long before Celeste decided that she had had enough of Geneva and was ready to depart for Paris. There were new fashions she wanted to buy and she had dog-eared many pages in Vogue and Harpers & Queen, her two favourite magazines.

Celeste was proud of her natural look. Most French women were, or so Vivienne thought. Parisian women dress for women. Not men. It is the women they want to impress. They want to be sophisticated, not sexy and preferred flat shoes to high heels.

Vivienne realised this rather quickly when spending time around Celeste or in Paris in designer shops or out dining in fine restaurants. Parisian women strived for a look that was admired amongst their counterparts.

From her experience with men, Vivienne knew that they wanted heels, stilettos and high-heeled boots. Most men – of course, there were always exceptions. Flat pumps in Paris were highly "de rigueur" and high heels are "de mauvais gout" (bad taste) so Vivienne was to realise. Vivienne was constantly chastised by Celeste for her heels and finally relented to wearing flats.

They arrived in Paris in late August, and Celeste began her shopping spree. Vivienne accompanied her and she watched as Celeste must have spent two hundred thousand in three days on clothes and accessories. Vivienne wondered when she would have the time to wear it all. Pastor would drive them to Montmartre or the Champs Elysees and wait patiently for them on double red lines whilst they shopped. Bags and bags of shopping would fill up the boot and still Celeste did not seem satisfied.

When the two women arrived back at the apartment, Victor was sitting cross-legged on the sofa in the drawing room watching television.

"Victor! *Mon tresor!* What a wonderful surprise!" Celeste seemed genuinely taken aback with Victor's surprise arrival. Vivienne was shocked. Victor stood, his beige chinos and white linen shirt fell open to reveal his stunning hard chest and his espadrilles revealed tanned feet. Vivienne was imagining him naked all over again and was glad Celeste could not read her mind.

"Look Vivienne. Victor has come to see us! How wonderful."

"Vivienne. Our own Vivienne." Victor came to her, his beautiful eyes looking longingly into hers. Luckily Celeste was standing behind him and did not see the longing in his eyes. Vivienne found it difficult to avert her attention away.

That night the three dined out at the George VI restaurant and Victor entertained Celeste with anecdotes of summer and gossip about the parents of his wealthy friends. Celeste was in her element, surrounded with two young people whom she adored. She plied them with drink and unfortunately Victor leant more and more into Vivienne, kissing her cheek and giving her far too much attention. This did not go unnoticed by Celeste.

"You two seem very close. Is there a spark there maybe?" this was a test from Celeste, not mild curiosity.

"Don't be silly Celeste." Vivienne pushed Victor's arm from around her shoulders and glared at him.

"How can anyone resist such a beautiful woman grandmamma?" Victor teased. He was going too far – the wine was getting to him.

Vivienne had to solve this before he ruined her job.

"Celeste. I think I might have my week off from tomorrow and go and see my family. Now that Victor is here, he can keep you company. Would that be acceptable to you?"

Victor glared at Vivienne. Celeste's face lit up.

"Yes of course you must see your family Vivienne. You take the private plane back to London and Victor will stay with me until he is due back at University."

"I have finished University Grandmamma. I sat my finals in June." Victor said flatly. He was not happy.

"Ah well. That's alright. Pierre can get you a job in the company." Celeste patted the back of Victor's hand with hers. Vivienne had won.

"Well, I might have plans of my own Grandmamma. I have plans to travel the world. A bit of backpacking maybe." He was so young. Of course he wanted to back pack. Vivienne was right to reject him.

*

As Vivienne packed that night, Victor entered her room without knocking.

"Where the hell are you going?" he demanded, turning Vivienne around to face him and holding her shoulders firmly. His beautiful face and passionate features tore through Vivienne's eyes and into her heart. *God how it was hard to push him away.*

"I'm sorry Victor. It has to be this way. I have a job to do here. You are my boss' grandson. It would never work. You are expected to find yourself and to grow, not marry your grandmother's private companion."

"That is my decision Vivienne. Not grandmothers" he took Vivienne's mouth then, and forced his tongue between her lips. Vivienne pushed him away reluctantly.

"I'm sorry Victor. It's my decision. Now please leave before Celeste finds you here. I am going to England tomorrow morning and it is over between us. Please understand that."

Vivienne did not know where she found the courage to say those words. She wanted Victor – *oh how she wanted him* – he would never know. Vivienne would be sacked and married to Victor. He would be cut off financially and he would soon hate her and Vivienne knew it would not work. She was looking out for him as well as for herself. His youth had not calculated the risks involved. Vivienne had.

"Please don't send me away Vivienne. Please. Let me stay with you tonight. Let me show you how I love you…." His beautiful pleading eyes filled with tears.

"No Victor. I am sorry. It has to be this way." Vivienne pushed him towards the door gently, and out. Closing the door on his beautiful, adorable face. Vivienne locked the door and fell against it. She cried as she sat on the floor. Vivienne truly loved Victor that night.

*

The next morning, Vivienne left for England. Celeste was tearful and told her to return as soon as possible. Victor was nowhere to be seen – he had gone out apparently the night before and still had not returned. He was making a stand against Vivienne, but it was no longer her problem.

"No doubt he has looked up one of his Parisian girlfriends and stayed the night." Celeste gleefully declared over their morning coffee. Although Vivienne did not miss the side glance from Celeste as the older woman eyed her carefully.

*

Vivienne left for England and to her family. She stayed with her parents in Berkshire and enjoyed the comfort of being back in the comfort and security of her home. Her parents listened enraptured over the stories of the Comtesse and the places Vivienne had seen.

Back in Paris, Victor had returned to the apartment. He had not wanted to see Vivienne's departure.

"Has Vivienne gone grandmamma?" he bent to kiss Celeste on her cheek.

"Yes dear. But don't despair. My masseur is on her way to look after me and I promise you we will both be entertained by her presence. Marlene always was an excellent entertainer."

Marlene sat in the Comtesse's jet. Vivienne had just left it and the engine was still running. The stunning brunette was on her way to Paris.

Marlene had heard of the Comtesse's sudden departure with Vivienne last winter and had presumed that the Comtesse had found out about the two of them. She had not heard a word from Vivienne and was desperate to see her. Marlene could not for a moment work out why Celeste would be prepared to see her again and had packed excitedly as soon as she was summoned.

She arrived at Rue de Courcelle's and was greeted warmly by Celeste.

"Marlene dear. So nice to see you – this is my grandson Victor..." Victor's mouth dropped at the sight of Marlene. She was wearing a tight, white leather dress which pinched her in all the right places. Her massive breasts protruded in a faux manner from her chest. Her long, dark curly hair fell down her back, longer than ever as her white, metal heeled sandals click-clacked across the marble floor towards him.

"Hello darling. So wonderful to meet you." Marlene kissed Victor on both cheeks. Victor was silent, unable to speak. He sat down on the sofa opposite Marlene with his legs wide open, staring.

"Put your tongue back in Victor. Marlene always has that effect on everyone, don't you Marlene. She has come to fix my back haven't you darling? She will be here for a couple of days." Celeste was up to her tricks again, she would punish Marlene and meanwhile, push her onto Victor to make sure there were no feelings from Victor towards Vivienne. No one could fool Celeste.

The three dined out at The Ritz that night. Marlene was wearing a floor length, bra-less, white lace skin tight dress. Her pink nipples escape sections of the lace and Victor was beside himself. He had trouble concealing his erection in his pants.

He could not believe Marlene, she was incredible. She was everything he ever dreamt a woman should be. He would have her. *He would have her*. That was all he could think about. Vivienne was forgotten.

Celeste had done her work.

*

That night after a nightcap, Celeste had taken Marlene to her rooms for a massage. Marlene stripped down to a white clinging bikini as she worked Celeste. Victor was in the next room.

Celeste was happy with her plan. Victor had melted at the sight of Marlene and could hardly speak at dinner.

"I want to talk to you about Vivienne, Marlene. I know everything that happened between the two of you. I want you to promise me that you will never see her again." Celeste spoke in a muffled voice, her face down on a towel as Marlene worked her back, pushing long movements into her spine. Marlene's movements slowed.

"Of course Celeste. I understand. You are in love with Vivienne, aren't you?"

"That is none of your concern Marlene. You are married. You concentrate on Gene and your business dear. Those are your only concerns." Celeste meant business, Celeste always meant business.

"Yes of course Celeste" Marlene massaged Celeste's back until the Comtesse fell asleep. Marlene left silently from her room.

Marlene retired to her room and took a long bath, the hot soap suds bouncing on her large breasts as they floated above the water line. She had purposely left the door unlocked, hoping that Victor would enter. She wanted him. He was a sight for sore eyes after months of hell with Gene and missing Vivienne like crazy. Victor was an excellent consolation prize.

There was a gentle tap at the door.

"Marlene. It's Victor. Can I come in?" he whispered loudly from the other side of the door.

"Yes!" Marlene replied – rapidly soaping up her breasts. "I'm in the bath."

Victor entered the bathroom with two empty champagne flutes and a bottle of champagne under his armpit, panting happily like a puppy.

"Why don't you join me?" Marlene suggested seductively.

Victor was out of his clothes in a flash and the champagne was forgotten as the two of them had sex in the bath tub, again on the bath mat and again on Vivienne's bed.

Celeste's plan had worked.

Chapter Twenty-Three

The Confession

Vivienne arrived back in Paris. Victor had gone back to New York. She was happy about this. She could not stand to watch his pain or even have the temptation of him around her. Celeste seemed in high spirits, more than Vivienne had ever seen her before. Vivienne thought this must be because she was back. She knew how much Celeste cared for her.

"My darling Vivienne. I missed you sweetheart. *Ma cherie.*" Celeste gestured for Vivienne to come and kiss her on both cheeks and tapped the sofa next to her.

"Tell me all about your week off. How are your parents?" this was formality, Vivienne knew that she was not interested in her family for one moment.

"Everyone is fine, thank you Celeste. So, Victor's gone back to New York?" Vivienne wanted to ensure there would be no further surprises.

"Yes. I sent him home yesterday. I have seen Marlene by the way. She came out here to fix my back. Victor seemed much taken with Marlene, I think the two of them became very close." Celeste dusted an invisible piece of fluff from her jacket. Vivienne was shocked. The bitch. She had planned it this way.

"Marlene was here?" *But, you hate her!*

"Yes. She is ever so good with her hands."

Vivienne could not berate her. She was already in trouble for the love letter she had received from Marlene, she knew she could not push it. It was not her place to question Celeste.

"Well. I am glad you are feeling better Celeste." Vivienne got up and went to leave the room.

"We have an appointment tomorrow on the Champs Elysees with the couturiers. There is a charity reception that we need to attend at the weekend and we have to look our best. There is also someone very important that I would like to introduce you to." Celeste opened her newspaper and pretended to be diverted by its contents. Vivienne stalled, and turned back to Celeste.

"A reception? What sort of dress is required?" Now Vivienne was curious. What did Celeste have up her sleeve this time?

"Long dress, evening gown. Royalty, film stars and politicians will be there and all the paparazzi, so your picture will be taken with me on the red carpet. That is all I can tell you. We have to find our clothes together so we don't clash." She threw the newspaper down onto the carpet as she would do when she had finished her paper and when she dismissed Vivienne.

Vivienne left the room bewildered. Celeste was not going to tell her any more than this – she knew her too well.

*

Later that evening Celeste was in good spirits and was already waiting in the salon with her customary aperitif. "Come and sit by me Vivienne. I want to talk to you." Celeste was unusually nice. Vivienne was always wary of her when she was this nice.

Vivienne sat down next to Celeste and she reached onto the coffee table and brought a black velvet box towards Vivienne.

"What is this?" Vivienne asked, genuinely surprised.

"Open it. Look." Vivienne opened the box and the largest tear- shaped diamond ring that she have ever seen, shone back at her. It must have been fifty carats in size.

"Oh Celeste. I cannot possibly accept this." Vivienne pushed it back to her. Vivienne felt she did not deserve it and also worried what the gift would mean.

"Take it Vivienne. I want to give it to you. You don't have to feel beholden to me for giving you such a gift, but I wanted to give you something to show you how much you mean to me. How much I truly love and admire you." There were tears in Celeste's eyes. She touched Vivienne's heart for a moment. But for only a moment.

"I can't Celeste. It would not be right," Vivienne whispered, imploringly.

"If you don't take this gift Vivienne, you will break my heart. You will probably break my heart anyway in time, but please do not break it tonight." She turned then, and closed the conversation. It was clear that Vivienne had to take it.

Vivienne did not try it on, but placed the box in her bedroom and returned to join Celeste for an aperitif. The two sat for while watching television, sipping a Saint Emilion until it was time for dinner.

*

That night Vivienne tried the ring on. It looked ridiculous on her finger, but fitted perfectly. The ring somehow made her feel more beholden to Celeste than ever.

Returning the ring to its luxurious box, Vivienne placed it into her bedside drawer.

*

That night, Vivienne was unable to sleep and finally gave in and got up at 2am to swim in the pool.

Stretching her legs and cooling her body, Vivienne washed Celeste from her emotions, from the guilt of her sad face, from the feelings of sorrow that Vivienne felt for the older woman.

Vivienne pitied her. She promised herself that night that she would never allow anyone to pity her in her life, now nor ever in the future.

It was the worst emotion that anyone could ever feel for someone else.

Chapter Twenty-Four

The exiled Prince of Persia

The Bois de Boulogne is a huge wooded park outside Paris surrounded by magnificent trees and parkland. It is a truly stunning area of outstanding natural beauty. Accessed by an avenue of trees is the famous Le Pre Catalan restaurant, frequented by royalty and the rich and famous.

The building is magnificent and is made of stone with marble, three stories high and has long, wide, delightfully bright windows from floor to ceiling. Inside, marble halls, mirrored panel doors imitating the Palace of Versailles divide the rooms. On the floors, thick black and gold custom made carpets and tables covered with white, damask silk table cloths and cream silk dining chairs covered in Louis XIV style silk.

Vivienne alighted from the Mercedes in a navy blue lace Alexander McQueen full length gown with a black sash around her waist. Her long blonde hair smoothed and twisted up into a large chignon. Celeste wore a black Chanel dress and jacket with grey lace border. She looked extremely elegant.

The two women were ushered into the grand reception room. People were gathering –it was a formal event to raise money for the homeless of Paris. At five thousand euros per seat and by invitation only. It was not acceptable to refuse the invitation and Celeste informed Vivienne that they had to attend. Vivienne had retrieved Celeste's cheque book from the safe in the Paris apartment. It was a huge cheque book, addressed to her Swiss bank account. There would be many cheques written that night in aid of charity.

"Someone very important is going to be here tonight Vivienne. His father was a good friend of mine and a very important person at one time. He was the Shah of Iran, the King of Iran. Unfortunately the poor man died and his son is the current exiled pretender to the throne. Anyway, I would like you to meet him. You will not have met such a fine example of a man until you have met Karim Mondegari."

"Karim Mondegari." The name rolled from Vivienne's tongue and sounded exotic and beautiful. Vivienne wondered what Celeste was up to this time. No doubt his match would be an exiled Iranian princess or some kind of exiled royal member who would have been extremely wealthy from a prestigious family like his. Vivienne could not imagine why Celeste was grooming her for such a presentation. Vivienne was dumbfounded this time.

*

Celeste was right. The first time Vivienne met Karim Mondegari she stared at him from the corner of the room. He was a beauty of a man. Tall, very slim, with black hair, dark chocolate brown eyes and relatively fair skin for an Iranian man. He had what you would call Ayran skin – almost white, yet with more of a European hue. He was seriously striking. His thick, slicked back hair was begging to have hands run through it. Vivienne was completely and utterly intoxicated. His features were strong, and his manners were impeccable.

His manner was unique to any man Vivienne had ever met. His eyes were piercing and all absorbing, yet full of kindness and gentleness.

He saw Vivienne from across the room and their eyes met. He watched her for a moment whilst talking to an elderly lady and eventually dismissed himself and made his way through the crowds to Celeste and Vivienne.

"Comtesse. It is an honour to see you again." Karim Mondegari clicked the back of his back heels together and bowed formally. His arms were vertically rigid in line with his body, his white gloved fists held tight. His dress was regal. His white suit had a long thick, dark red stripe on the outside of each leg panel, and a royal blue satin sash over his right shoulder. Gold threaded epaulets balanced on each shoulder and his chest was covered in medals and a solid gold medal was placed in pride of place around the yoke of his chest. A long sword was placed on one hip with a sapphire, emerald and ruby studded handle protruding up to his waist line. Vivienne had never seen such a vision of beauty and elegance. There were other royalty in the room, Vivienne recognised them all, but none were dressed like Karim Mondegari.

Unfortunately for Karim, he was the only King in the room that was not allowed to sit upon his own throne, except for Celeste of course. Vivienne's heart went out to him and his family for being exiled from their own country, never to be allowed to visit ever again. Many exiled Kings had chosen to live in Paris, including our own abdicated King who instead of staying King to England, preferred to marry his twice divorced lover, Wallis Simpson, which almost brought down the English throne. Love. It appeared to have many powers – even beyond duties of Kingship.

"Karim. May I introduce my ward, Miss Vivienne Lawrence." Karim Mondegari turned to Vivienne. His full attention on her face as he took her hand and kissed the back of it three times.

"It is an honour to meet you Miss Lawrence. We have a custom in Iran to kiss three times. Of course, I am not permitted to kiss you on your beautiful cheeks, so I kiss your hand instead. Forgive me." He bowed again, clicking the back of his heels and Vivienne melted.

"You are very kind Your Excellency. Thank you." Vivienne was almost stunned for words.

"Do you come here often?" Vivienne stammered. *What the hell?*

Thankfully, Karim Mondegari felt Vivienne's awkwardness and smiled.

"On occasion only. I prefer the comfort of my own home in Montmartre." He replied politely, covering over Vivienne's obvious slip-up and embarrassment. His dark brown eyes were like melted chocolate, his long angular nose, narrow features, and beautifully kissable pink mouth smiled at her. Vivienne smiled back. She did not talk, but listened to Karim's polite small talk with interest. Celeste was busily chatting to other guests.

"How long have you known the Comtesse?" Karim asked, he took a long look at Vivienne, taking in her exclusive gown.

"For about a year your Excellency." Karim took two glasses of champagne from a passing server and offered one to Vivienne.

"Champagne?" His eyes glistened and Vivienne saw a deeper more natural side of the man than the costume he wore.

"Thank you." Vivienne took the glass and they both sipped silently. She felt his gaze and uncomfortably looked away for a moment, but his conversation brought her back to him immediately.

"Do you like Paris?"

"Yes your Excellency, very much. Although I miss England." Vivienne admitted.

"Yes. I understand this problem. I miss my country also, I was very little when my parents were forced out of their own country." He looked away for a moment and appeared to be picturing the very moment. Vivienne felt awful that she had mistakenly brought back such a painful memory.

"I am sorry your Excellency. That was very thoughtless of me."

"No. No. It is not a problem. It is a fact. I have had to live with it, but I wish things could be different." He sighed then and Vivienne felt she had intruded on his personal thoughts. He appeared very charming and she was warming to his sense of patriotism. He loved his family and his country dearly, that was clear to see.

"And when do you return to England Miss Lawrence?" Karim changed the subject.

"Well. Very soon I think. Maybe in a week or two?" Vivienne said this as if it was a question, as she truly did not know.

"Ah, I see. The Comtesse has a hold over you, no? She decides when it is time to return." Vivienne knew what he was thinking, and it worried her.

"Yes. Something like that." Vivienne was worried that he knew more about the Comtesse than he was letting on and wondered how much he actually *knew* the Comtesse.

"My mother was very close to Celeste when she first came to Paris. She knew no-one and Celeste knew everyone. Celeste is very close to our family and we are indebted to her generosity and kindness. Any friend of Celeste is a friend of mine." He smiled at Vivienne again, a suave, sexy smile. Vivienne was lost.

"Thank you your Excellency. That is very generous of you." Vivienne meant more. His voice was gentle and elegant. He had a way of caressing with his smiling eyes. His teeth were even and square and relatively short, but perfectly formed in his mouth. His mouth was wide and full and his nose Arabic in places with a slight hump which was the only imperfection on his face but which provided him with enough ruggedness to make him pleasing to the eye. His hands were masculine and strong, yet delicate and controlled. He handled everything he touched with gentleness and poise. He was well educated and thorough with every aspect of his personality.

"Now look, if we are to be friends, you must call me Karim and may I call you Vivienne?" he voice sounded like velvet and his thick Iranian accent pronounced Vivienne's name in an exotic manner.

"Thank you...Karim. I would like that." Vivienne smiled and genuinely felt she had a made a friend.

"Now excuse me Vivienne, I must be sociable tonight otherwise everyone will think I am taking you for myself and that would not be fair, now would it?" he kissed Vivienne's hand three times once again and she watched as his gentle mouth fluttered over the back of her hand. Vivienne could feel the heat of his breath on her skin and instinctively her hand covered in goose pimples. She pulled it away embarrassed.

"Let me take you back to Celeste. Where is she? Ah, there she is, talking to The Sultan of Brunei. Come my dear."

The rest of the evening was a blur as Vivienne was introduced to royalty, famous film stars and politicians from all over the world. The evening was a tremendous success and three million euros were raised for the worthy cause. During the late supper, Vivienne sat next to Celeste and further down the table, she could see Karim. Next to Karim, a far older, rather large woman was talking animatedly. He listened attentively whilst staring at Vivienne during the entire dinner. Vivienne felt his gaze bearing down on her and if she blushed, which she never did, she was sure she did that night.

Vivienne was in trouble, she knew it. She was falling potentially in love with a King. An exiled King admittedly, but someone with whom she probably could not have. *Shit – why did her life have to be so complicated?*

Chapter Twenty-Five

La Soiree

A few days after the reception at the Bois de Bologne, they departed for England. Vivienne was glad to be home. It had been a long hot summer. Victor had asked her to marry her and she had been tempted, but knew it wasn't right for either of them.

Marlene had confessed her love to Vivienne and so had Celeste. Now, there was Karim. She felt sad leaving him behind in Paris and that the chances of seeing him again were unlikely. Maybe next summer.

Vivienne sighed as she unpacked her things. She did not want Matos to unpack them this time, she wanted time alone, away from Celeste to think of Karim. Celeste had chatted constantly on the flight home.

*

Vivienne felt as if her life was not really going in the direction she wanted these days. She would have to check her bank accounts to see if she had saved enough money to leave Celeste. She felt guilty that she thought this way as Celeste had been very generous and kind to her. But, in truth, Vivienne was there because she was being paid to be there. She wasn't Celeste's companion for the fun of it. It was work after all and Vivienne had no life of her own. She could never decide what she wanted to do next, or where she would like to eat or go on holiday. Celeste made all these decisions.

Vivienne's life had not been her own for nearly four years and she knew that her goal for saving for a future life was getting closer and closer. She thought again of Karim. He had taken her breath away with his beautiful formal attire, but she knew that that wasn't the real Karim and she longed to see what he would wear in clothing of his own choice. Vivienne imagined him in bleached jeans with holes and a scrunchy linen white shirt, opened at the chest, like Victor would wear and laughed. She wondered if he had hair on his chest or whether it was clean shaven. Vivienne smiled to herself for thinking such things and loved to imagine him in all kinds of scenarios away from the one they had met.

Vivienne thoughts were interrupted by the house telephone in her room and she knew it would be Celeste. She picked up the phone.

"Vivienne speaking." She tried not to sound exasperated.

"Ah, Vivienne dear. I have some work for you. Please could you come up to my office?" Celeste sounded as if she had a thought in mind, another plan that she wanted to involve Vivienne in.

Silently and swiftly Vivienne left her quarters and climbed the wide stairs to the first floor. Celeste was sitting at the desk in her office as she entered. She was wearing a pretty mauve linen dress with matching pearls around both wrists in a cuff like affect. She was always dressed impeccably.

"Ah there you are Vivienne. Now. It is time to plan my Centenary Charity Ball and of course I need your full attention to help me plan it. I have a guest list here, there are three hundred. I want you to take this down to Mount Street and give it to Ian. He will be responsible for inviting them all and ensuring they attend." Vivienne glanced at the list. Her eyes scanned down…His Excellency Prince Karim Mondegari. Vivienne nearly screamed out in delight. Holding her thoughts, she left Celeste and went straight to Mount Street to see Ian McAllister.

*

The receptionist stood when Vivienne entered. Vivienne had not seen the miserable woman for nearly four years since her interview. It was never necessary for her to go to Head Office. Ian always came to see Celeste religiously once a week for an update report on the business, usually over dinner and several bottles of exclusive red wine.

The receptionist stood immediately and smiled. Her demeanour was respectful and welcoming. Completely different from the first time Vivienne had met her.

"Hello Miss Lawrence. My name is Julie. I am Ian McAllister's secretary. Anytime you need anything, you just call me and it is done." *What a turnaround.*

"Hello Julie. Is Mr. McAllister around? I have an important errand from her Excellency," Vivienne informed and the young girl totted off down the corridor.

Ian McAllister quickly arrived carrying his bulky weight in large strides across the carpet.

"Vivienne. How lovely to see you. You have a message for me?" he took both her hands and shook them warmly, the guest list almost scrunched in her hands.

"Come. Come this way, my office is down here." Vivienne followed him to a back office, it was masculine with burgundy leather sofas and armchairs filled the room. A mahogany desk with a burgundy leather baize top stood in pride of place. He lifted a pile of papers from the visitors chair opposite his desk and placed them onto another equally messy table and offered Vivienne a seat. Julie entered.

"Can I get you a cup of tea or coffee Miss Lawrence?" She spoke very precisely and was keen to take another look at employers' private companion. She gazed at Vivienne, looking her up and down and admired her designer suit and Jimmy Choo shoes.

"No thank you Julie. I am due back to her Excellency's in a moment and will take tea with her." Vivienne glibly replied. Julie had been very rude to her and she would not forget it.

"Thank you Julie, you may go." Ian McAllister ushered her away and shut the door behind her. Vivienne found this action unusual as there was nothing that Julie could not hear that she had to report about Celeste.

"How can I help you Vivienne?" Ian McAllister sat down at his desk – he was sweating a little.

"I have a guest list for the Centenary Charity Ball. The Comtesse wanted me to give it to you. Is there anything else that I should do?" Vivienne handed the list to Ian. He glanced at it through his glasses and rubbed his mouth and chin with his hand.

"Mmmmm. Yep. Okay. Nothing too unusual there, although some of them maybe out of town." He declared. Vivienne was suddenly worried. She knew that Prince Mondegari was in Paris.

"Ah….those that are not in London, do they usually attend?" Vivienne enquired carefully.

"It depends. If they have business here in England or have a home here, they may make an effort and attend." He had not looked up at her and was still eyeing the list, moving down each name with his forefinger. He stopped about half way down on the second page.

"Mmmm. Prince Mondegari…."

"Ah yes. Doesn't he live in Paris?" Vivienne enquired gently.

"Yes. Although he also has an apartment here in Chelsea." This piece of news was music to her ears and Vivienne carefully shifted in her seat with anticipation of the invitation being accepted.

"And…who will be responsible to ensure all the invitations are sent out and accounted for?" Vivienne enquired.

"I will. I cannot entrust this task to anyone else." Ian McAllister informed her, quite soberly.

"Ah I see. I could oversee this, if you are busy that is," Vivienne added carefully.

"Now don't you worry your head with such business Vivienne and concentrate on looking after our boss. That is something that I cannot do as well as you." He stood now to end the meeting.

"Thank you for bringing the list to me. I will ensure everyone gets an invitation." He finished.

"Will there be another list of acceptances to follow?" Vivienne pushed.

"Yes of course. This will done within the next fortnight hopefully. I will bring it round to Grosvenor Square when it is finalised."

"Don't forget what I told you Vivienne. Don't forget who you are."

"Right. I'm off. I've got to attend on the Comtesse." Vivienne left then, hastily. Ian McAllister knew how to upset her and was good at it. He had a hold over her. He knew her background more than anyone and felt he could send her back there anytime he wished. Well he could not. He was no longer in control of her destiny.

Vivienne would make sure of it.

*

The day of the Charity Ball at Grosvenor Square soon arrived and the staff busied themselves all day with preparations. Caterers had entered via the back garden and taken over the kitchens. A team of waiters and waitresses were being trained up by Matos who was showing them the house and grounds. Vivienne bumped into them on her afternoon rounds and one of them curtseyed to her in their black and white waiter's attire. Vivienne found this rather amusing and went to watch the early evening news with Celeste before they both retired to make themselves ready for the ball.

At seven o'clock Vivienne and Celeste were both ready. Celeste had chosen a shimmering gold creation by Chanel which hung in long folds down to her feet, ending in a fishtail affect.

"Vivienne darling. You are a vision sweetheart. You are a beauty in the Dior. I was right. It suits you perfectly."

Vivienne smoothed down the front of her white lace creation. A tight white dress clung to her body and stopped at the top of her thighs and then over the top, a layer of lace tightly fitted over her bodice and arms and hung in see-through folds to her feet. It was elegant and yet fashionable and slightly daring. Vivienne had liked Celeste's choice and if anyone dared to tell her it was 'too much', Vivienne would simply tell them that Celeste had chosen it. After all, she was the fashion Icon of the century.

Guests began to arrive and Celeste was the perfect hostess. Smiling and greeting everyone. Karim arrived and Vivienne watched him this time, from the far corner of a room. She was cornered by an elderly gentleman who declared he owned most of Texas. His breath stank of bourbon and he wore a Stetson proudly upon his head.

Fortunately, Vivienne was able to hide behind it and watched over his shoulder as Karim worked the room. He was moving gracefully, making small talk and moving on, not stopping to talk in detail with anyone in particular. He appeared to be searching for someone. He was wearing his formal attire once again and looked stunning, this time, a white jacket with the blue sash and black trousers with the burgundy stripe. He was indeed stunning and the tallest man in the room.

He found her then, but not before Vivienne had a chance to look back to her Texan and pretend to be captivated by his conversation, laughing at a remark. She felt Karim's gaze on her as if there was a light shining over her. Vivienne could feel him moving steadily towards her and she made sure that she did not glance in his direction.

Vivienne knew that in order to catch the prince, she would have to be very cool.

"May I interrupt?" His deep voice flooded her world. The Texan turned and glanced at Karim. He appeared annoyed to be interrupted.

"Well hello there your Honour." Vivienne cringed at the inappropriate address to Karim and stifled a giggle.

Karim rudely ignored him and bowed to her, clicking his back heels together. The Texan removed his hat, scratched his head and put it back on. He was quite put out.

"Miss Lawrence. It is an honour to see you again." Karim's eyes pooled over hers. Was there a glimpse there that he might, just might, feel the same way as her?

"You're Excellency. How wonderful to see you again. Lance, this is his Excellency Prince Karim Mondegari." Vivienne announced proudly.

"You're Excellency. This is Lance Granger of Texas." They shook hands and the Texan was not pleased to be introduced at all.

"So, where are you Prince of?" Lance rudely enquired.

"Iran sir. Exiled." Karim offered in a short response.

"I...Ran." "Bad subject where I come from. We don't talk about I...Ranians." he put in bluntly and turned his back away. Poor Karim probably had a lot of this to contend with. Vivienne felt ashamed that she had entertained such a racist idiot.

Vivienne walked away from the Texan and Karim followed her.

"Is there somewhere we could go?" Karim whispered into Vivienne's ear.

Vivienne took him down to the conservatory and out into the garden. The late September air was mild and the garden was lit up with glass lit lanterns. They sat down together on a wooden bench under a pergola of roses that were still in full bloom.

"I'm sorry about Lance." Vivienne put in. The silence was long. Karim had talked little since the rude Texan.

"I don't care about the Texan. I came home to Chelsea because you were here Vivienne. No other purpose. I was waiting for a reason to come to see Celeste. Now I have one. I am so happy to see you again." His eyes reflected in the moonlight and the whites were shining and true. Vivienne believed him.

They talked about his family. About his father. He was the son of the dead Shah of Iran, Mohammad Mondegari. His mother and sister still lived in their home in Chelsea in London. They were not allowed to live in their native Iran. Their country was run by Muhler's or Priests, so-called elected by the people, but this was not true – those who did not vote for the enforced rule would be hung publicly in the streets. The people wanted their country back, the people wanted their King back.

"The palaces are closed now. There is graffiti on the walls, the summer palace in Shiraz is just an empty shell, a museum. I remember it as a beautifully quiet place. It has a wonderful shallow pool, lush green gardens and cool long marble corridors. It is a haven in the heat of summer."

Vivienne could tell Karim missed his home terribly. He had only been eleven when he was forced to leave with his family. His father could not take the humiliation and pressure and died shortly after. A tear welled up in his eye and Vivienne could see that painful memories returned. Her heart went out to him.

"My ancestors were the first kings of the world and ran the first Kingdom, well before the Egyptians. They worshiped fire and still the fire temple or at least its ruins stand near Persepolis. For five thousand years we were kings of our own lands, all to be overthrown in 1975."

He talked with passion of Persepolis, the temples of the old kings that worshipped fire and told Vivienne of the majestic palace there, much of it destroyed by Alexander The Great and much also stolen and taken to other countries.

"I would love to show you Persepolis Vivienne. At night we hold operatic performances and light shows which are breath-taking." Vivienne listened attentively to his stories, staring at his hard features speaking soft words of memories and his home. His voice was melodic, comforting and delightfully erotic to her mind.

He stopped talking then and stared deep into her eyes, he found understanding there and compassion. Vivienne smiled back.

"You are a rare thing Vivienne." He said her name in a slow pronounced way. It sounded exotic spoken from his tongue. Vivienne smiled and put her head down shyly. How she loved Karim to say anything to her that would perhaps demonstrate that he had feelings for her.

Vivienne only wished that Karim might feel the same way that she felt for him.

"I would love to show you England – true England. England is not London. London is the city – it is politics and business. It is not England. "

"I would love that Vivienne. You would show me these things?" he said endearingly. We were becoming friends fast and Vivienne hoped that he would be able to see the real Vivienne amongst all this pretense that Celeste put on – the grandeur of impressing all the time – this was not her.

"You are different to Celeste, Vivienne. You are not the same at all – why do you work for her?" *the million dollar question.*

"Because she pays me Karim. I do not have an inheritance or money of my own. I must earn it."

He blushed then, he knew only too well. Vivienne saw that Karim felt a little ashamed that he had not worked this out for himself.

"Of course Vivienne. Forgive me. Such a stupid question. You see, you seem so graceful, so elegant, so far removed from all of this nonsense – you are a very wise woman – we say in Iran – an old woman on young shoulders – this is how I see you – except your shoulders are beautiful- you are very beautiful Vivienne – you remind me of an English rose. Delicate, sweet and pure. You are too good to pick Vivienne. Are you too good to pick?" He held her chin up then with his thumb and forefinger and she thought he was going to kiss her. Vivienne was very still, afraid to speak. Not wanting to break the spell of the moment.

"I can only be picked once, then my petals start to fall." Vivienne whispered gently.

"Exactly so. Exactly so." He leant in towards her and took in her scent, ever so subtly.

"You smell so sweet, like a beautiful rose in full bloom." He uttered.

"You are very eloquent with your words Karim. Do you read poetry?" Vivienne asked.

"Poetry. You know in Iran we have the most famous poets and some even more famous who have been dead a long time and their burial places are places of worship."

"What are their names?" Vivienne swallowed. She wanted him to kiss her. She didn't want to talk.

"Hafez. Saadi. They wrote the most romantic poetry that is in existence. Do you know in Iran we have ten ways of saying 'I love you' and 'you are beautiful'?

"May I kiss you Vivienne?" his lips were so close to hers.

"Yes." Vivienne whispered lightly, he would not have heard her say it, but felt the word on his lips.

Karim kissed her then and she melted into his arms. All the years of pain and sorrow were washed away as she felt his warmth and tenderness in that one kiss. His mouth moved gently and smoothly over her lips and she felt his tongue ever so gently flick inside her mouth. He grew a passion inside of her that she had never known to exist until now.

Vivienne felt a love deeper than she had ever felt before Karim. *Karim. Karim.* His name was her mind and entering her very soul, step by step. Second by every beautiful, heady second.

Sadly, the party was coming to an end and she had spent far too much time with Karim in the garden. They were chilled when they re-entered the house and were just in time for the coffee trays. They sipped silently as Celeste chatted happily with her guest. Ian McAllister came over to Vivienne. Karim moved away.

"*Don't forget who you are Vivienne…*" he added. Vivienne turned to look at Ian and swore to herself that that would be the last time he would ever say that.

The guests left one by one and Karim was last to leave. Ian hovered around the dying canapés.

"Celeste. What can I say? What a tremendous night. Your charity will be happy with your funding from such a successful event, well done." Karim hugged Celeste and kissed her three times, first on her left cheek, then her right and then her left once again.

"May I come and visit you soon?" Celeste was taken aback and then glanced at Vivienne. Vivienne was waiting, perhaps a little too interested in his reply.

"Ah. I see what is happening here. Yes, yes, of course you may, of course Karim. My house is your house. You know that." She squeezed his two hands and Karim kissed Vivienne gently on the hand in front of Celeste, slowly. She could feel Ian staring into her back. *How she hated that man.*

Chapter Twenty-Six

Revenge is Sweet

The next morning Celeste was full of joie de vivre as flowers and glorious bouquets arrived in their dozens from guests who had enjoyed a wonderful night of entertainment. Once again, Celeste was queen of Mayfair and within hours invitations came flooding in for soirees all over London and abroad. Two boxes took Vivienne's interest in particular. They were both from His Excellency, Karim Mondegari.

One was addressed to Celeste with one hundred pink roses. Vivienne removed the note to give to Celeste along with all the others. The other box was addressed to Vivienne and she was surprised that no one had mentioned this to her before. Inside the box were one hundred red long stemmed roses with the thorns carefully removed to ensure she did not hurt her fingers. The card read:

For the belle of Mayfair: Vivienne

These roses are a small token of the affection and respect I hold for you – you were a success and a credit to Celeste.

I hope to see you very soon.

Affectionately yours,

Karim x

Vivienne smelt their sweet scent. Karim's choice of flowers were perfect and simply presented in a white rectangle box with raffia ribbon holding the stems in place. Vivienne knew that red meant passion, which made her smile. She had hoped that they would be more than just friends. Rosa was running around trying to sort out the bouquets, she had more flowers than she knew what to do with. Fortunately, most of the bouquets had arrived in water-filled arrangements.

"Shall I take these roses Miss Vivienne and place them in a long vase?" Rosa inquired as she saw that Vivienne had taken a particular interest in the display.

"Oh would you Rosa? Could you put them in my bedroom?"

"Of course Miss Vivienne" Rosa left with the box clutched in her arms which over-shadowed her small frame.

Vivienne found Celeste in her bedroom eating a late breakfast tray. They had not had their customary walk around Hyde Park that morning which would often not take place after a late night of entertaining.

"Ah Vivienne…there you are" Celeste almost berated, but contained herself. Vivienne wanted an opportunity to speak to Celeste about Ian. She had not forgotten the last encounter with him the night before. Vivienne placed the cards she had taken from the bouquets and placed them on a space on Celeste's side table, keeping the one written by Karim for herself in a pocket in her dress.

"Have you seen all the flowers that have arrived for you Celeste? There is enough to fill at least four florist shops!" Vivienne had a knack of changing the subject when Celeste gave even a hint of negativity, which was often.

"Rosa told me, I am sure they are wonderful." Celeste did not demonstrate interest and Vivienne could see that her passion for many things these days were fading. It was sad to see.

"Celeste. I have something sensitive that I would like to talk to you about, if I may?" Vivienne suggested, carefully.

"What is it? What's the matter?" Celeste was suddenly on guard and put down her spoon. It was the first time Vivienne had ever asked of Celeste's time or demonstrated a concern for anything.

"It's about Ian..." Vivienne began.

"Ian? What about him? Has he upset you? That silly old fool. What has he done now?" Celeste said this in such a way that made Vivienne question if Ian had perhaps upset a previous companion of Celeste. Maybe this wasn't the first time.

"He keeps saying something to me that I feel is unfair and unwarranted. I have put up with it for a long time now, but I feel that I should bring it to your attention," Vivienne carefully suggested.

"What is it Vivienne? What does he say?" Celeste took Vivienne's hand and encouraged her to speak.

"Whenever I see him or am alone with him he says *"don't forget who you are"*...I have spent nearly four years trying to figure out what he really means by this...but he always says it in a manner of control or threat." Vivienne stated.

"Mmmmmm. I see. I will speak with him Vivienne. Do not worry. He will not say it again." Celeste patted Vivienne's hand and Vivienne smiled appreciatively. She did not want to ask Celeste what Ian might have meant by this statement...it could have meant a number of things. She would leave Celeste to make of it as she wanted – just like Vivienne had for the past four years.

*

Celeste picked up her house phone and called through to Mount Street. Ian answered the phone almost immediately.

"Celeste...how wonderful to hear from you. The charity ball was a great success last night. Well done." As usual, Ian knew how to pander to Celeste.

"Yes. Yes. I am calling about something else Ian. I am not happy Ian. Not happy at all," Celeste stated flatly.

"...wha..." Ian began.

"No...do not speak Ian. Do not interrupt me. Vivienne has expressed a concern about something you apparently keep saying to her – and I won't have it Ian...do you understand? Vivienne is not like the others, I will not have her made to be upset in any form – now are you quite clear? If this happens again Ian I will have to take certain measures to ensure it will definitely never happen again. Are you quite clear on what I am saying Ian?" She was quite clear.

"Of course Celeste. I apologise. Whatever I have done to offend Vivienne, I sincerely apologise," Ian stammered.

"Yes well, it's not me you have to apologise to you silly old fool, it's Vivienne and make sure it is done today – do you understand?" Celeste instructed – slammed down the phone and left a bewildered Ian looking in the hand receiver. *Apologise to Vivienne. What a nightmare.*

*

Vivienne was sorting through her clothes deciding what needed to go to the dry cleaners when Matos came knocking at her bedroom door.

"Yes?" Vivienne echoed. Matos opened the door.

"Ian McAllister is here to see you Miss Vivienne." Matos stated.

"Tell him I will be right there Matos, thank you" Vivienne was thrilled. Celeste must have called up to the head office and berated Ian. *Vivienne was going to enjoy this.*

Vivienne changed calmly and slowly into a formal suit. She would make him wait. Wearing her straightest face, she entered the salon twenty minutes later. Ian was waiting impatiently.

"Ah Vivienne. So nice to see you…" Ian stood up to greet Vivienne, but Vivienne just sat down.

"Hello Ian. How may I help you?" Vivienne asked flatly.

"Well. I think there must have been a misunderstanding between the two of us. If I have in any way offended you Vivienne, I strongly apologise…" He was stammering and sweating profusely. Vivienne was thoroughly enjoying herself.

"Good. Celeste has made it clear to you that I am not replaceable. Some of us might be Ian, but I can assure you I am not and I will not be spoken to in such a degrading manner.

Once, you interviewed me for a position. I was a different girl back then and naïve. I am no longer that girl Ian and certainly no longer naïve. I will not be treated in such an undermining manner. Do you understand?" Vivienne was repaying him for the insults of the past four years.

"Of course Vivienne. I apologise and hope that you can forgive me." Ian rose then as if to close the meeting. Vivienne had not closed the meeting.

"Sit down Ian. I have not finished," Vivienne ordered. Ian sat down sheepishly.

"I want you to be clear about the relationship I have with Celeste. It is one of equal respect and friendship and nothing more. Do you understand? If you assume that I am anything like she has had before, you are quite wrong and personally I take it as an affront of my honour

222

that you could suggest that I might be anything less than this. I can only assume that your repetitive statement to me was an implication that I might be something worth far less." Vivienne was determined to clear the air.

"No. No. Of course not Vivienne. I would never suggest such a thing." Ian had his head down and Vivienne had never seen the man act so humbly. Their relationship had changed forever from this day forward.

*

Celeste never asked Vivienne if Ian had apologised. The question of Ian's behaviour was never mentioned again. Celeste had enough authority to assume that once she had raised a query and put forward her demands, it would be sorted.

Vivienne was irreplaceable and that was that. Ian was now aware of this fact and over the coming weeks and months learned to respect Vivienne in a different light than he had before. The girl had turned into a beautiful, graceful woman who no man or woman could challenge.

Chapter Twenty-Seven

Oyster Bar, Harrods

It was hard after the charity ball to forget Karim even for a moment. He occupied Vivienne's thoughts night and day. She wondered why he had not come to visit as he had promised. She began to have trouble sleeping, eating and sometimes even talking and entertaining Celeste. If the older woman noticed any change in behaviour in Vivienne she did not remark upon it, but respected her space and her own thoughts which Vivienne was grateful for.

Celeste had accepted for a long time now that she would never conquer Vivienne in the way that she had desired and hoped.

Vivienne busied herself as much as she could, waiting for Karim to contact the house.

One early afternoon during Celeste's siesta, Vivienne decided to take a cab to buy another pair of running shoes. Although the pair she had were only a year old, they had taken a thrashing and were looking a little sorry for themselves.

Vivienne entered Harrods and headed for the escalators and the sports room. She walked down to the trainer section.

Vivienne stood in front of the rows and rows of colourful trainers, when she heard a distinctly recognisable voice. It was high-pitched, demanding, bossy and loud. It could only be Marlene. Vivienne had not seen her for a year.

Marlene stopped in her tracks when she saw Vivienne, she too was coming to buy a pair of trainers, although Vivienne knew she had hundreds of pairs.

"Vivienne, darling. How wonderful to see you. Where have you been, you naughty thing, have you been ignoring me?" She was as gorgeous as ever in a tight, white weave sweater and white leggings. She wore an incredibly high pair of white platform shoes with pathetically thin straps. Her long red painted toes nails spilling over the edges.

"Hello Marlene. So lovely to see you. How are you?" Vivienne worried the old passions would return to her with Marlene standing there in all her loveliness, her breast bulging and her lips swollen, but thankfully the woman no longer had any effect on her. Vivienne at last could say that she was no longer in wonderlust of

Marlene. At last, she was over her and for that she was truly thankful. Thanks to Karim.

"Oooo, no, don't buy those darling. They won't last. Nike. Only Nike. Trust me." Declared Marlene. Good old Marlene. Always full of advice, whether you wanted it or not.

"Let's have lunch sweety. My treat."

Vivienne had no choice but to accept and the trainer she was holding was ripped out of her hand as Marlene pulled her towards the escalator.

"Let's have some oysters and champagne darling. Celebrate the good old days." Marlene was as hedonistic and as over-controlling as usual and Vivienne wondered what she had ever seen in her.

They arrived at the ground floor oyster bar in the Food Hall and Marlene elbowed herself a space for herself and Vivienne. People around stared in curiosity at these two contrasting women, one blonde and tall and the other brunette and sexy. Together they were a dynamite duo.

"Did you get my letter?" Marlene had turned unusually serious. Vivienne realised that the best thing to do was to pretend that she had not received it.

"No. What letter?" she lied.

"Ooooh. That bitch." Marlene swallowed two oysters whole, one after the other and leaned towards Vivienne.

"How do you put up with that conniving bitch? She must have stolen the letter I wrote you. No wonder she dragged me to Paris and got that grandson of hers to seduce me. That cow." Marlene was spitting anger now.

"She did what?" Vivienne could not believe it. Victor had fallen for Marlene as well. Victor was staying at Celeste's when she had left for her family break and Marlene must have been on the return flight that brought her to England. The two of them probably had sex in her bedroom in Paris. Vivienne felt like vomiting and the oysters no longer looked appealing to her.

Everything made sense now. Celeste was so jealous of her that she had used Victor to entice Marlene from her. Well, she needn't have bothered. Vivienne was deeply and irrevocably in love with Karim. She had never truly been in love with Marlene, lust maybe.

With Victor, it had been a wonderful diversion for a while – he was far too young and too spoilt to interest Vivienne.

She didn't mention Karim to Marlene. She didn't need to know and she could no longer trust her. Vivienne would have to steer clear of her in future.

"Ah. Look at the time. I must get back to Celeste. Her siesta is almost over. It's been lovely Marlene. We should do it again sometime." Vivienne kissed her on both cheeks and before Marlene could object, ran out of Harrods and stepped into a waiting cab.

Chapter Twenty-Eight

Kings Quay – Chelsea Harbour

The next morning by coincidence or pre-arrangement Vivienne was not sure, Karim arrived unexpectedly at the house in Grosvenor Square. She heard him talking to Celeste in their typical jovial way as she walked into the salon at the front of the house.

"Well it's the gorgeous Vivienne" Karim was as fabulous as ever dressed in a fine merino wool navy blue suit with a pristine white shirt open at the chest, wearing no tie and appeared relaxed.

Vivienne had never seen him without formal attire and he looked even more stunning in casual stress.

"Hello your Excellency." Vivienne hated being formal with him, but it had been a long while since the charity ball and he had not been in contact.

In truth, Vivienne wanted to run into his arms. Instead he bowed politely to her. He was close enough for her to smell his aftershave. He filled Vivienne's nostrils with musk, sandalwood and something like a fresh fruit, maybe a watermelon. It was a different perfume to the one he wore at the charity ball and in Paris. His olive skin glowed and shone and a slight matting of black hair escaped his muscular chest. Vivienne found it hard to avert her gaze from him.

"Where have you been to get such a great tan?" Celeste enquired and Vivienne waited for his answer in trepidation.

"St. Tropez. We have a villa down there – you should come sometime Celeste and of course with Vivienne." He said sincerely in his educated American tilted Iranian accent reaffirming the invitation when he looked longingly in Vivienne's direction.

Vivienne breathed a sigh of relief. She thought his feelings had changed towards her and that he had attempted to keep a distance to break the bond between them. Just one look. One longing look. That was all it took to confirm to her that he still had feelings for her.

"Let's have champagne shall we?" Celeste clapped her hands in excitement and Lourel came running in on his short little legs.

"A rosé Louis Roederer Champagne please Lourel." Lourel shuffled out and brought back a chilled bottle of the vintage champagne and the three drank to being back together again.

Vivienne had not been so happy and relieved in a long time.

"So I have decided to take the two of you out tonight as my way of saying thank you for such a wonderful party Celeste, Vivienne." Karim held up his glass in salute.

"Oh Karim. You are such a gentleman. We shall love that, won't we Vivienne dear?" Celeste was in her element.

Lourel came back into the room. Celeste glanced up at him, expectantly.

"Your Excellency. Ian McAllister is here to see you on an urgent matter." Celeste became suddenly downcast and partially frustrated at having her little party rudely interrupted.

"All right Lourel. Send him to my office will you?" Lourel shuffled back out of the room.

"Darlings. I will have to love you and leave you, but just for a moment I hope."

Celeste left the room and Karim and Vivienne were quite alone.

"I have missed you Vivienne." Karim leaned over to Vivienne and touched her hand. After a moment, he moved to sit closer to her.

"I missed you too Karim." She wanted to berate him for not calling the house or sending a message that he would be out of the country, but she knew she could not. He was a prince after all. One did not order a prince around.

"I wanted to call you, or send a note – but I thought it might compromise your situation here – perhaps..." Karim attempted to explain himself.

"You are right Karim and I appreciate your thoughtfulness, I truly do." Vivienne meant it, she already had experience of Marlene's letters being interceded. Vivienne was still unsure how Celeste would take it if she knew how Vivienne felt about Karim or if they became anything more than just friends.

Suddenly, Celeste walked back into the salon and Karim quickly removed his hand from Vivienne's and moved quickly away. The action was not missed by Celeste, although her mannerisms showed no displeasure.

"I am sorry my darlings, it appears my business will take some more time that I had thought. Look – Karim, why not take Vivienne out for me, but please bring her back at a reasonable time." Celeste gave a warning look over her glasses to Karim which were still perched upon the bridge of her nose from an important document that she had just been looking at.

"Of course Celeste. Vivienne is in safe hands – I promise you." Karim had stood and held Celeste's hands together with his own in an affectionate manner. *God he was smooth.*

"That's exactly what I am worried about." Celeste admonished. She smirked over Karim's shoulder at Vivienne and left the room.

*

The Connaught Hotel was an old gentleman's club and decorated in fabulous mahogany wood panelling and surrounded with green parlour palms. Karim and Vivienne were welcomed and taken through to the Connaught Bar, an ultra-stylish décor. The room was surrounded with 1920's Irish art, with textured walls shimmering in platinum silver leaf overlaid with dusty pink, pistachio and lilac.

Several people seated stopped to watch the two enter. Vivienne and Karim made a handsome couple, Vivienne knew it and she hoped that Karim felt it too.

Karim led her to a quiet table behind a parlour palm and away from prying eyes.

He ordered a bottle of champagne and leaned forward and took Vivienne's hand.

"You look very beautiful tonight Vivienne. I can honestly say I have never met a more beautiful and striking woman as you."

"Thank you Karim. That is a great honour." Vivienne blushed and her heart began to beat faster. She was excited to be with Karim. He was without doubt the most charming and beautiful man she had ever met. She adored him more and more, but there was a fear inside of her. She knew she was at risk of having her heart broken if she did not step carefully. Karim would not be an easy man to have a relationship with.

"I can feel that we will be great friends, you and I." Karim pressed. Vivienne just smiled and took a sip of her champagne. The whites of Karim's eyes sparkled as he rubbed his jaw, a habit she realised that he constantly undertook, especially when he seemed a little nervous.

"Is there something troubling you Karim?" Vivienne asked. If there was something that she needed to know, the sooner she knew about it the better.

"No. Of course not sweet Vivienne. I have much experience with the opposite sex. I have been brought up by a very loving mother and a doting sister. I am very comfortable around women." Vivienne smiled at him. This was not the answer she had hoped for – he was being evasive.

"There is no doubt that your beauty and my feelings for you make me a little nervy Vivienne. That is the truth, you are beautiful and I want to make a good impression on you. But enough about me. Tell me about your childhood, your family, and your dreams. I want to know all about Vivienne."

Karim had cleverly changed the subject and Vivienne was not about to press him further so told him what he wanted to hear. He listened intently. He seemed to be far more comfortable in listening rather than talking about himself.

Vivienne desperately wanted to know more about him, but she knew that most of his life story was full of painful memories of leaving his adored home country and so politely, she did not return the question. In time, Karim would talk more about his family and his life when he was ready.

*

Karim dropped Vivienne back to Grosvenor Square at a reasonable 11.30pm and Celeste had already retired to bed. Vivienne took a leisurely bath and thought about her time spent with Karim. He had held her hand whilst she had talked about her childhood and experiences, in particular a funny anecdote experienced during her time living in South Africa which made him laugh. His hand although far bigger than Vivienne's, had been warm, loving and sincere. His manner was gentlemanly and refined. Vivienne was genuinely impressed by his elegant manners and he had left an impression in her mind that she knew would sit in her heart for a long time to come.

The next morning Vivienne woke to a letter that had been pushed under her bedroom door.

Dearest Vivienne,

You have captured my heart and I must see you again, to hear your voice, your laughter and to stare into your beautiful blue eyes. The eyes where I have drowned many a night dreaming of you. I will be at home all evening, please come to me for dinner. Just dinner – I promise.

Riverside Penthouse, King's Quay, Chelsea Harbour.

From your faithful friend and servant,

Karim Mondegari

Vivienne held the note in her hands. She wondered how it had been sent to her without interception. It was written on thick embossed A5 cream paper with a black border. She smelt it. Karim's sandalwood scent emanated from its intricate weave.

She went to her wardrobe to select an outfit suitable for a date with a King without raising suspicion from Celeste. She chose a Maxmara Sport black dinner suit that she could wear without any top underneath, just a black bra and buttoned tightly with a pair of black Manilo Blahnik sling-backs. She put the outfit aside for later.

*

Celeste was busily sifting through letters when Vivienne approached her in her study. She was beautifully dressed as always and wearing a navy blue and silver woven Chanel suit. A long platinum and sapphire necklace spilled onto her papers as she leant over them, studying them meticulously.

"Excuse me Celeste. May I have a moment of your time?" Esther trotted over to Vivienne from one of her many beds and Vivienne bent to acknowledge her. She licked her fingers appreciatively.

"Yes Vivienne. What is it dear?" Celeste's tone sounded languid and uninterested.

"If it is not inconvenient, I would like to pop out to see an old girlfriend tonight." Vivienne hesitated. She was a terrible liar and hoped Celeste had not sensed her discomfort in disguising it.

"What friend is that?" Celeste's face was still down reading her papers.

"Carly. My best friend. I haven't seen her for quite a while now," Vivienne lied. She had popped out only two weeks previously whilst Celeste had her siesta. Carly and Vivienne had met for drinks at a local Mayfair pub and caught up on their girly gossip.

"You should bring her here Vivienne, to meet me." Celeste looked up at Vivienne and directly into her eyes – her hands had been placed in a folded position and she closed the folder containing her papers, offering Vivienne her full attention. Vivienne felt extremely uneasy. She felt like she was asking her sergeant major for time off from duty.

"Ah. Well. The plan is that I drive to her house in Hampshire. Maybe another time?" Vivienne suggested as an alternative.

"Very well. Make sure you tell Matos so he can let you in later. I assume you will be coming home tonight?" She enquired. Still staring directly at Vivienne.

"Of course Celeste. I will walk out with you as usual tomorrow morning," Vivienne promised.

"Fine. I shall entertain myself. Maybe I will call Karim to take me out." *Damn.*

*

Vivienne dressed with great care that evening. She creamed her body with scented oils and put on her new La Perla underwear that she had bought which was in a delicate black lace. She painted her toes and nails and washed and brushed her hair until it shone. She applied a little makeup and sprayed just a little shower of perfume into the air and stepped into it, so as not to take too much intensity.

*

Vivienne arrived outside Karim's penthouse at 8pm. A respectable time to arrive she thought. She entered Riverside at Kings Quay and the grand marble reception was huge with parlour palms and a doorman welcomed her. The opulence of the building was modern and impressive.

"I am here to meet His Excellency Mondegari – Riverside Penthouse?" Vivienne enquired, rather hesitantly.

"Your name please Miss?"

"Oh sorry. Of course. It's Vivienne Lawrence," Vivienne added, forgetfully.

"Yes Miss, please take a seat while I call up to the house."

Vivienne was too nervous to sit down and hovered away from the desk, tapping her fingertips on her clutch bag.

The doorman picked up the telephone on his desk and pressed a few buttons.

"It is Harold on reception sir. I have a Miss Vivienne Lawrence for you waiting in the lobby sir – shall I send her up?" the doorman hesitated for a moment, waiting for an answer. "Yes, Sir. Very well sir, thank you sir." He replaced the receiver.

"This way please." The doorman showed Vivienne to the lift and ushered her forward. Taking a key from a long chain of keys on his hip, he placed one of them into a slot labelled 'Penthouse Suite' and turned and released the key and pressed the button.

"Thank you Miss. His Excellency will receive you at the top."

The doors closed. Vivienne was quite alone. Inside the lift, gold and black ebony mirrors surrounded her. After a few minutes, the doors opened.

Karim greeted her with a warm hug and kissed her on her cheeks, the customary three times.

"Vivienne. I am so pleased to see you. Welcome to my humble home."

He took her coat and clutch bag and placed them on a side table. The hallway was magnificent, the black marble floor and oversized lit chandelier glowed in unison with each other. A black shiny grand piano graced the far corner. Persian silk rugs were placed lavishly over the floors and a more detailed pure silk carpet hung on one wall. Since they had met, Vivienne had been studying the Koran and the laws of Islam to try better to understand Karim. As she looked at the silk carpet on the wall she recognised the face of the prophet Mohammed. Vivienne was only too aware of the differences in their religious beliefs and culture, let alone the fact that Karim was an exiled King. *She sure knew how to pick 'em.*

"Don't worry. We are quite alone. My housekeeper doesn't work at weekends and my man servant has been given the night off."

Vivienne was not sure whether to be relieved or disappointed. Although she was sure that she was perfectly safe in Karim's company alone.

Riverside was a luxurious six- bedroom penthouse apartment on the banks of the River Thames, in the heart of Chelsea, with 7,600 square feet, and views towards Cheyne Walk and the harbour. It had a formal drawing room, a family room with open plan kitchen and informal dining area, formal dining room and separate chefs' kitchen, a music room, study, games room, wine storage, gym with spa area, as well as five luxurious bedroom suites including a palatial master bedroom suite with terrace on the river, with additional separate staff quarters.

*

"Come. Let us have some champagne in honour of your first visit. You are a very important guest here tonight."

Karim moved forward and leant in very close to her. He took her hand and kissed it whilst staring into her eyes. Vivienne's stomach somersaulted. He really knew how to woo a woman.

He turned her hand over and kissed the inside of her palm, then reached his hand out to her face where he held her cheek for a moment and then kissed the place on his hand where he had just touched her. This action would soon be a gesture that would become very close to Vivienne in her heart.

"May I kiss you Vivienne?" Like Victor, his manners were impeccable. Karim was such a gentleman. She melted just watching his features soften.

"Yes," Vivienne whimpered, pathetically.

Karim drew her into him them and embraced her. His lips firmly, yet smoothly moved over her mouth, with such conviction and yearning she melted into his embrace. She was sure she was going to faint. The combination of the champagne, hardly any food that day and a gorgeous olive-skinned, dark haired Prince embracing her was a heady combination.

*

It wasn't long before Karim was carrying Vivienne to his bedroom. Dinner was long forgotten and left on the dinner table where his housekeeper had set it all up lovingly.

Karim made love to Vivienne with great tenderness and affection. She truly felt loved in his arms more than she had ever felt in her entire life.

Karim stared into her eyes as he entered her.

"Look into my eyes, azizam and see how much I love you," he spoke.

Vivienne wondered what 'azizam' meant, but knew it would be something adorable knowing Karim. Their affair had progressed rapidly. Too rapidly. She knew this. But the hours they could spend in each other's company were minimal and he knew as well as she, that at a moment's notice, Vivienne could be flown off again by Celeste.

There were no regrets. None at all.

Karim kissed every inch of her body, appreciating her curves and loved her more affectionately than she had ever been loved before.

"A woman such as you should never be neglected my love. Never. I would cherish you and adore you every day of your life if you were mine." He breathed as he worked over her body.

Vivienne delighted in his touch. He was an incredible lover. He did not exert expertise, but from being able to love deeply from within his heart.

Vivienne felt she had been given exclusive access to Karim's soul, through his eyes and his mouth. She was sinking deeper and deeper into his world and she knew she might never be the same again.

*

Later they sat in bath robes and ate their supper hungrily, laughing about house designers and the extraordinary items they chose to use which were often totally hideous and uselessly expensive.

"What does *azizam* mean Karim?" Vivienne asked shyly, remembering the moment with a smile.

"It means *my love* in Farsi, which is my language, the language of the Persians," he stated, proudly.

"Beautiful. I like it. You should teach me some Farsi Karim, I would like to learn," Vivienne added, seriously.

"Of course azizam. I would be happy to teach you?" He smiled at her then and stopped eating whilst he stared at her in puzzlement.

"You are making me feel uncomfortable now, stop staring at me!" Vivienne covered her face in embarrassment. Those deep dark eyes were disturbing to her. They seemed to tear open her soul and search deep within her and drag out every single thought and secret that was held there.

Karim was intense. Vivienne had never known a man or even a human being like Karim before. He was mysterious. He was magical. He was amazing.

They made love again. Less passionately this time, yet more intensely and they fell asleep naked in each other's arms.

*

At dawn, Vivienne rose leaving a heavily sleeping Karim in his luxurious bedroom with his thick black hair tousled over his forehead and his left arm flung over his face. He looked young and adorable in his sleep. His torso was still naked and the black curly matting of his chest hair glistened in the morning light as the sun rose, casting shadows across his bedroom. Vivienne was tempted to jump back into bed with him, but it was a risk she was still not prepared to take, and she had promised Celeste that she would be there for their early morning walk.

The sun was just rising as she poured herself a coffee and lent over the balcony in Karim's penthouse suite.

Down below on the harbour she saw a stunning, cherry wood yacht with a sundeck and sails.

A *For Sale* sign was tied to its mast representing Foxton's Estate Agency. Retrieving her mobile from her clutch bag on the hall table, Vivienne tapped in the number and saved it.

In her hand she held her sling-backs so as not to wake the sleeping Karim and kissed him goodbye on his cheek, careful not to wake him.

Outside Karim's building, she hailed a taxi and managed to get back to Grosvenor Square just in time.

Chapter Twenty-Nine

Scarlet Nights

Back in her bedroom in Grosvenor Square, Vivienne sat at her dressing table, playing with a set of hair pins, lining them up like soldiers.

Vivienne knew she would have to make a plan to leave Celeste eventually. Things could not carry on as they were. Eventually, Celeste would find out about Karim and destroy that relationship too. Vivienne didn't think she could bear that. She truly loved Karim and she thought he felt the same way too.

Vivienne was struggling to cope with the intensity of Celeste's life and needs. Vivienne was tired of pandering to the woman.

She was fed up of dining out in fine restaurants every day. She wanted to wear jeans, walk Esther, go on a bike ride, and walk in the countryside with wellington boots. Kiss Karim. All of these things were not possible living and working with Celeste.

She had to think of a plan. She had to think of it fast, before she lost Karim. Someone like Karim would not allow a woman like Celeste to control his life.

At the first, Vivienne had been blown away. The job was the best thing that had ever happened to her and for that she would be eternally grateful to Celeste, but the older woman wanted more. She wanted to own Vivienne.

Vivienne missed her own home and a simple life with no servants. She had enough money for sure, but the money was not the motivation any longer. She truly did not want to hurt Celeste.

*

One early autumn morning, Vivienne told Celeste that she needed a hair cut, and it was true, she did. She had an appointment with Nicky Clarke, but not until much later. Soon she would be returning to mainstream hairdressers for her cuts as she would not be on an expenses allowance for much longer.

She had called Foxton's Estate Agency and made a plan to visit the yacht on Chelsea Harbour. She found a riverside café and ordered a cappuccino and put a £10 note down on the table.

Vivienne smiled ironically at her first visit to Richoux and the coffee that she could hardly afford. She had managed to turn her life around in these four years. She had done very well for herself, but at a personal and emotional cost.

She would never be the same innocent person that she had been then. Vivienne was a stronger person now. Additionally, she was no longer intimated by wealth or wealthy people or impressed by what they owned or what they wore. Most importantly, she had also managed to finish her degree and no longer felt intimidated by educated people.

*

'Scarlet Nights' was a gorgeous 1920's yacht. It was sixty foot in length, with a wheel room and a sun deck made in a soft glossy cherry wood. It was in pristine condition and Vivienne marvelled at it whilst she stood waiting for the agent.

A cute looking man in his late twenties turned up with his long hair backcombed high over his head and gelled down. Two little bobby clips held his hair in place behind his ears which Vivienne found quite enchanting. He wore a tight stylish Italian suit, and well-made Italian leather soled, pointed shoes. He was not at all what Vivienne was expecting.

"Nice to meet you Miss Lawrence, my name is Jack Goodacre. Nice boat isn't it?" he looked her up and down and tried to judge her wealth by her clothes. He did not miss the Cartier watch on her wrist or the rock balancing on Vivienne's right finger. He reached out to shake her hand and in the other he held a clipboard, pen and a glossy brochure of the yacht they were about to view.

"I am absolutely taken away by this boat. How much is it?" Vivienne knew that if you had to ask the price of something, you could not afford it. Celeste had taught her this, but in her case she had no time to waste on pleasantries.

"Well. Shall we take a look inside first?" Jack Goodacre smiled, ushering Vivienne onto the boat.

"This yacht is an excellent opportunity to explore the waterways in opulent style" he began. *Little did he know that Vivienne could not actually sail.*

"As you can see, there are original 1920's features throughout and modernised in some areas like the kitchen for example. Period details are evident inside and out, while both the superstructure and infrastructure have been well maintained since a full restoration has been carried out by the loving owners." *Well if they loved it that much – why were they selling it?*

"The interior is dominated by cherry wood and brass, resulting in a refined atmosphere throughout, whilst the accommodation itself encompasses in excess of five hundred square foot of comfortable living quarters."

"The yacht has three bedrooms. Two bedrooms at the rear end, and at the fore-end a cabin with double bunks, a saloon lounge which can also be converted into a double bedroom, a wood panelled bathroom, a separate toilet and the benefit of abundant storage. There is also lots of secret nooks and crannies throughout." He was opening and closing compartments. Vivienne stifled a giggle. *She would give him ten out of ten for effort, although he needn't have tried so hard as she knew she was going to buy it.*

The salon was very inviting with a fitted sofa in soft cranberry velvet spreading around the room against a cherry wood panelled wall and fitments custom-made for the yacht. In the centre of room, there was a beautiful large glass coffee table with a huge display of white lilies in a large clear glass bowl which reminded Vivienne of Grosvenor Square. *Funny.*

The recognisable and beautiful aroma filled her nostrils with their glorious floral scent.

He climbed the steps to the deck and urged Vivienne to follow him.

"Externally, the deck has recently been re-seamed, whilst the present owner has added a sun lounge at the stern providing an area that is perfect for al fresco dining or a bedroom under the stars!" he was really enthusiastic about this boat.

"How much are the mooring and licence fees?" *Ah, ha, he had forgotten to mention that.*

"£10,000 per year all in" he added – he had left that out purposefully.

"The yacht is a steal at half a mil' – but I think the chap who owns it is open to offers" *good, because that figure is fifty grand over my budget.*

"Great. Okay. I have £450,000 cash. Tell the seller to take it or leave it!"

"But, don't you want me to start the engine?"

"No. It's okay. I can't sail. I will live in it here."

Vivienne offered Jack Goodacre one of her white and gold embossed calling cards, turned and left.

"Call me when you have some news for me." Vivienne called out without turning and left Jack Goodacre standing on the boat.

*

On the way back to Mayfair, Vivienne made her hair appointment just in time and while she sat under the professional hands of Nicky she thought about the beautiful yacht she had just seen.

Vivienne wanted that boat. She needed that boat. It was a perfect demonstration of freedom that she so desperately needed to escape Celeste. It was all she needed. Nothing more. Only perhaps, Karim to end the perfect fairy tale.

'Canon' by Pacobel sung from inside her handbag and became louder and louder. It was her mobile.

"Hello?" Vivienne's said expectantly. She rarely received anonymous phone calls these days.

"Ah Miss Lawrence? It's Jack Goodacre. I have some great news. The vendor has agreed your price based on a cash sale with a completion in four weeks."

"Fantastic news. Well done Jack." Vivienne's voice lifted and she felt wonderful.

"I will call my solicitor and have him contact you. No problem to the four weeks, we can arrange that." Vivienne did not know who the 'we' was. It just sounded less pathetic and lonely.

"Great. I look forward to hearing from your solicitor then. Congratulations on your purchase Miss Lawrence, I am sure you will be very happy sailing up and down the River Thames!" *he had forgotten that she couldn't sail.*

*

"Ah – there are you are Vivienne. Your hair looks lovely darling."

"Thank you Celeste – what are your plans for tonight?" Vivienne never asked this question, but her time was becoming more and more precious to her and she had a plan now, and Celeste would be the last to know it. If ever.

"I am not sure dear. Maybe we'll stay in and dine here tonight, is that alright with you darling?"

"Of course Celeste. Whatever you want" Vivienne sat down on the sofa next to her in the salon. Celeste was watching the French news channel on television. Once again, it had been wheeled in front of her, the cables spreading across the floor.

An advert came on the television for urgent money needed in Africa. Children were dying of poor water quality and urgent donations were requested by the Red Cross.

"Terrible. Terrible." Mumbled Celeste.

Vivienne picked up her mobile which she had never used in front of Celeste before and dialled the number on the television screen. She donated a thousand pounds.

"What did you do that for Vivienne? The company takes care of all that." Celeste turned back to the television and changed the channel.

Vivienne suddenly did not know the woman she had worked for all these years. Vivienne was shocked. The next thing Vivienne said shocked herself even more than it did Celeste.

"If you don't pick up the phone right now and give a substantial amount of money to that cause, I will pack my bags right now and leave." Vivienne was cool, clear and quite calm and Celeste could see she was deadly serious.

Celeste looked at Vivienne. For the first time in four years she looked terrified. She said nothing to Vivienne and reached for the telephone.

"Ian? Yes, it's Celeste. There is an advert on television for the Red Cross for water purification in Africa. Yes? Well, send them £100,000 pounds and ensure they have enough to fix the problem will you?....I know, I know – but just do it – okay?" she commanded. She hung the phone up and looked at Vivienne.

"Thank you Celeste. It means a lot." But it did not. It was too little, too late. The disappointment of the woman had left its mark on Vivienne.

Chapter Thirty

Karim's Proposal – early winter

The next day Celeste has risen earlier than usual and left the house for a private meeting with her doctor. She often crept out without notice when visiting Harley Street, never wanting to go into detail about one concern or another. Vivienne knew Celeste was paranoid about her health, overly so and if someone sneezed over her by mistake, she would take a shower and make an appointment to see her doctor the following day.

Vivienne was sitting quietly in her private lounge reading a magazine when the external house line rang out. Vivienne never picked up an external call. It was extremely rare that a call would be for her anyway and it was not her place.

"Excuse me Miss Vivienne. There is a Karim Mondegari on line one for you." Matos bowed and left the room.

*

"I want to have a private discussion with you Vivienne" Karim was deadly serious.

"Yes of course Karim. What is it?" Vivienne had no idea what the nature of the urgency could be.

"I have a proposal for you. It is important that you take me very seriously."

Vivienne swallowed. She was quite still, not wanting to breathe. She pinched herself to ensure she was not dreaming.

"My dear darling, have you no clue whatsoever how I feel about you?" he breathed heavily down the telephone.

"We should not talk on the house phone Karim." Vivienne interjected. She had a picture of him, his gorgeous deep brown eyes and dark lashes with thick eyebrows that almost met in the centre of his forehead.

What he said next made Vivienne's world fall apart.

"You know I have to marry an Iranian woman. My mother has found someone for me. She is alright I suppose, although of course, she is not my choice." The phone line was silent. Vivienne's heart sank. *Why on earth did she think he was going to ask her to marry him?*

"Karim. I truly don't understand where you are going with this conversation. What on earth does this have to do with me?"

"I don't want to lose you Vivienne. I am madly in love with you." He sounded desperate. All Vivienne could think about was that the conversation was being taped.

"I want you for my own, but I cannot offer marriage. I will buy you an apartment in Chelsea, close to mine and I will spend as much time with you as I can. I want to steal you from Celeste. Tell me you will come to me instead." *Instead? What was I?*

"You insult me Karim. I am deeply insulted." Vivienne choked back tears. It had been four years since she had cried over a man and she did not want to start again now.

"Surely what I offer you is far better than what Celeste is offering you?"

"No Karim. You want me to be your secret mistress which would mean I would never be allowed to be seen out in company with you." Vivienne began to cry. Tears were falling from her face.

"My darling. Please, please do not cry. If I had things my way I would marry you. You are my choice."

"Then what are you afraid of Karim? Choose your own life – don't make others choose it for you."

Vivienne admonished. She was especially frustrated as she had tried to convince Victor of the exact opposite.

"You do not understand the way of my culture Vivienne. What you ask of me is impossible for me to give. It is not mine to give." He was silent again.

"It does not matter anyway Karim. I am in love with someone else," Vivienne threw in proudly.

"What? Who? You never meet anyone. Who can this person be?"

"It is not who you expect. It is Marlene Forsythe. You have never met her. She was Celeste's private fitness instructor and masseuse. We met through Celeste. It is complicated. Anyway, we are in love with each other." Vivienne choked out – finally not caring if the telephone was taped or not. She was insulted. She no longer cared. Everyone would know that he had hurt her.

"You cannot be serious Vivienne, after what we have shared together. Marlene is not good enough for you. She is a whore and a person without morals. You are worth more than that."

"She is magnificent. She is unique. She is my passion. I don't expect you to understand, but I do adore you too Karim. I have always respected and adored you. You are a beautiful man and my interest in you is no different than any woman that would look at you."

"Are you trying to tell me that you are bi-sexual Vivienne?" Vivienne did not know whether he was disgusted or curious. Maybe a bit of both. Vivienne was hurting him, as he had just hurt her. He would not use her like Celeste, Marlene or Victor. Vivienne would not be used again.

At last she knew why Celeste was not worried about Vivienne and Karim's potential relationship. The old woman had known that he had a pre-arranged marriage.

Karim hung up and Vivienne was left staring into the mouth piece of the telephone. After a few minutes the house phone rang again. Once again, Matos entered the room.

"There is a Karim Mondegari on line one for you Miss Vivienne." Bowed and left the room.

"I don't know what to make of this Vivienne. This is not something I have ever come across before. This is so bloody western. What is wrong with you? Can't you just be normal?

"Normal Karim? What is normal? Do you consider taking a mistress and marrying someone you don't love normal?" Vivienne spat back.

"It is a matter of honour Vivienne. It is what is expected of me!" he admonished.

"Honour? You call taking a mistress behind your wife and your family's back a matter of honour?" Vivienne rose from the sofa, she was too angry to sit.

"I don't need you or anyone to buy me an apartment in Chelsea Karim. Anyway I have my own plans. I don't need you or anyone to be a personal slave to!" Vivienne whispered sharply down the telephone to him.

"Vivienne, Vivienne, darling. Don't let us hate each other." He sighed exasperatedly. Vivienne did not want to leave on bad terms with Karim. He was a good friend, although she had hoped it would be far more.

"Can't we just be friends Karim?" Vivienne pleaded, her heart breaking. She knew the call was going nowhere. Karim had made up his mind.

"No Vivienne. How can I be friends with a woman I want to kiss every inch of, that I want to be inside of, that I want to hold and to spoil and to cherish and to fill her with my undying love – tell me that?" his voice sounded choked. Vivienne could hear him crying.

"I understand Karim, but what you offer me is not good enough for me. If I were to accept your offer, you would not be honouring me and above all, I would not be honouring myself."

Vivienne did not think that Karim had ever received a rejection in his life. He would have been idolised from a young age and idolised by women who were desperate to be in his company let alone marry him. Karim had genuinely thought that his offer was a good one and that Vivienne would jump at the chance to be his mistress. She was not that kind of woman. She had never been that kind of woman and she was not about to become one now.

"I am sure you can respect me for my decision Karim. But my answer is no. Thank you, but no thank you. I have to go now, I have work to do. Goodbye Karim." Vivienne was silent for a second or two.

"Not goodbye Vivienne. Never tell me goodbye. Until next time." He hung up the phone. Vivienne allowed him that. It would have been rude to hang up on a King after all. For a moment, Karim had lost his pride, his honour and everything he ever stood for – *for just one moment.*

Chapter Thirty-One

Esther – winter

Vivienne slept restlessly that night. In the morning she entered Celeste's rooms and the older woman was in relatively good spirits.

Vivienne was still feeling upset about her opinions two nights previously and she knew it would stay with her for a long time. As far as Vivienne was concerned enough was never enough for starving, dying children. Celeste and Vivienne obviously had a difference of opinion.

More and more Vivienne realised how far apart the values of her employer and her own were. Vivienne no longer wanted to be part of this system. She had made her mind up, she had come to say 'goodbye' to Celeste.

"Celeste. I need to talk to you." Vivienne stated flatly.

"Yes Vivienne, what is it dear?" she put down her newspaper and took off her glasses.

"I have decided that it is time for me to leave." Vivienne waited patiently for Celeste's reaction. It was not what she expected.

"Of course Vivienne dear. You must do what you feel is right for you.

Celeste leant over to a small box and retrieved a carefully folded piece of paper. It seemed to have been left there for a while.

"I want to give you something. It is a cheque to change your mind Vivienne. If you decide to take it, you can come back to me and we will not say another word about it."

"I have taken enough from you. I don't want anymore," Vivienne said, honestly.

"Don't be silly Vivienne dear." She handed the cheque to Vivienne. "If you decide not to take it, I will understand and I hope that we shall be friends and you will come to see me from time to time." A tear had appeared in the corner of her eye. She was putting on a brave face.

"This is very difficult for me Celeste. I have toyed with the idea for a while now. I truly don't want to hurt you, but I cannot go on like this anymore, I am very sorry." Vivienne was being as honest as she could. She truly did not want to hurt Celeste, but it seemed unavoidable.

"You must follow your dreams Vivienne dear. It has been fun." Celeste put her hand up to Vivienne's cheek and held it there, staring into her eyes. She pushed the cheque into Vivienne's hands.

"Now, go now. Be happy, with my blessing." She was being brave. Vivienne expected that the older woman had had to be brave many a time with matters of the heart.

Vivienne leaned in to her and kissed her on her cheek, Esther jumped off the bed and came round to lick Vivienne's hand – the little dog seemed agitated. She knew something was wrong.

Vivienne got up and left, without turning back. Her conscience would not allow her to look back at Celeste's face. She could not see the pain she had caused there.

*

In her room Vivienne gathered all her belongings and called Lourel to take them to her car. He seemed surprised, but did not ask her any questions. He truly was the perfect butler. Matos had left to see his family for his annual holiday to Goa. Vivienne would miss him. She did not have the chance to say 'goodbye' to him so she left him a note on her dressing table and another simple one for Rosa for her excellent house-keeping.

Dear Matos

I never knew your first name and forgive me for never asking it but I was just doing my job. Hopefully I will see you again one day, but in the meantime I would like to say 'thank you' for taking care of me and watching over me ☺ Take care

Vivienne x

Vivienne walked up the steep path behind the Georgian mansion house with her flight size suitcase in tow and two suit carriers over her shoulders, Lourel carried the rest. Esther came running up yapping behind her like she always did when Vivienne was due to leave on a break.

Esther barked and dragged her feet and claws across the grass border of the path as if to say "you can't leave yet"....poor little thing. She would miss her terribly.

Vivienne put down her bags and allowed the little dog to jump into her arms. Vivienne whispered into her ear, talking gently and stroking her to calm her, telling her how much she loved her and that maybe in their next life, she could be her dog.

Esther was absolutely still and silent as she cocked her little head to listen and the tops of her furry pointed ears twitched in understanding of what Vivienne was saying. Vivienne told her to be a good little dog and to look after her mistress.

Vivienne placed her onto the path and she sat immediately, patiently, politely, almost in understanding and hopelessness, her little head slightly tilted to one side.

Vivienne peered down into Celeste's bedroom which overlooked the garden on the ground floor. The curtain twitched and finally parted and there Celeste stood, standing solemnly at the window. Celeste understood that it was time for Vivienne to leave. She would no longer stop her.

Vivienne picked up her bags again and with one last look and a blow of a kiss to Esther, she turned and pressed the intercom exit button and the thick steel gate clanked as the bolt was released automatically and Vivienne left.

Behind her, Vivienne could hear the whimpers of Esther. They became louder and louder and Vivienne had to clear her throat loudly in an attempt to try to block out the sound.

The beeper of her car alarm signalled her Mercedes was now unlocked as she placed her baggage into the boot. She got into the driving seat and sat.

Esther was now howling. Vivienne had never heard her howl before. She didn't even know a Yorkie could howl. Vivienne started up the engine and turned up the music to drown out the sound.

But. She couldn't leave.

Vivienne turned off the engine and got out and went to press the external intercom. Lourel answered.

"The Laisalle residence, can I be of service?" Lourel's repetitively trained voice droned out.

Vivienne was free now, but he was not. He would not see his family for another eleven months and that was if he had worked hard enough and grovelled sufficiently enough to Celeste for his annual leave.

"Lourel – It's Vivienne" she breathed. Vivienne had never called herself to the staff by her first name out of respect for each other's positions and in respect of the protocol that ran in the house without question. Esther's howling had now stopped and the poor little dog was crying and scratching at the bottom of the steel door.

"Miss Lawrence. Of course. How can I be of service to you?" he prattled in his usual thick accent.

"I forgot something – sorry – this is the last time you will have to put up with me saying that!" Vivienne said, convincingly as the bolt unlocked.

Vivienne pushed open the door; it was heavy and always required two hands to push it. Esther was there, she had stood back waiting for the door to re-open and looked up at Vivienne in anticipation, unsure what to do.

"So Esther. Who is it going to be? Celeste or me?" Vivienne said as the little dog tilted her head and whined.

Then, the little dog did something incredible. She turned her head and stared for a while down at Celeste who was looking forlorn from her bedroom window. The dog and her owner held each other's gaze for just a moment. Esther was saying "thank you, but I want to go with this lady."

Esther turned back to Vivienne and jumped into her arms and the two left. The heavy steel door shut automatically on its spring and the bolt shunted into place.

Vivienne placed Esther on the passenger seat and retrieved the cheque that Celeste had just given her and read it. It was written out in Celeste's hand for £2,000,000, a parting gift from Celeste or more of a bribe to stay with her? Vivienne was not sure.

The poor woman couldn't even pay for Vivienne to stay. Vivienne had only pity for the older woman now.

Vivienne ripped up the cheque and reversed out of the mews garage and headed towards Fulham Broadway and Imperial Wharf where '*Scarlet Nights*' was moored.

THE END